W9-CEA-049

HAPPILY EVER AFTERLIFE

Drama

by Orli Zuravicky

SCHOLASTIC INC.

HAPPILY EVER AFTERLIFE

To my sisters—
Dori, Shiri, and Darya—
my afterlifelong friends forever

Text copyright © 2017 by Orli Zuravicky

All rights reserved. Published by Scholastic Inc., *Publishers since 1920.* SCHOLASTIC and associated logos are trademarks and/or registered trademarks of Scholastic Inc.

The publisher does not have any control over and does not assume any responsibility for author or third-party websites or their content.

No part of this publication may be reproduced, stored in a retrieval system, or transmitted in any form or by any means, electronic, mechanical, photocopying, recording, or otherwise, without written permission of the publisher. For information regarding permission, write to Scholastic Inc., Attention: Permissions Department, 557 Broadway, New York, NY 10012.

This book is a work of fiction. Names, characters, places, and incidents are either the product of the author's imagination or are used fictitiously, and any resemblance to actual persons, living or dead, business establishments, events, or locales is entirely coincidental.

ISBN 978-1-338-19299-5

10 9 8 7 6 5 4 3 2 1   17 18 19 20 21

Printed in the U.S.A.   40
First printing 2017

Book design by Jennifer Rinaldi

SHAKESPEARE UNIT

Ms. Elizabeth Barnard
English I, all sections

Play: *Twelfth Night*, a comedy by William Shakespeare (1564–1616)

Summary: Twin siblings Viola and Sebastian are separated in a shipwreck. In the village where she washes ashore, Viola disguises herself as a boy and becomes the servant of the rich Duke Orsino. Orsino is in love with Countess Olivia, who falls in love with Viola (in her male disguise). Unknown to Viola, Sebastian arrives in the same village later, and, looking so much like Viola in her disguise, causes confusion and hilarity!

Objective: To perform this play for the school two weeks from today! You may either audition for a role or sign up to help backstage. Everyone must participate, as this production will count for 100% of your grade in this unit.

Auditions will take place this afternoon at 4:00.

Be not afraid of greatness:
Some are born great, some achieve greatness,
and some have greatness thrust upon them.
—William Shakespeare, *Twelfth Night*

Chapter One
Upstage(d)

So . . . you may already know this, but I'm going to just come out and say it right from the start so we can get it out of the way and move on to more important things.

I'm dead.

Yup, D-E-A-D. Dead. Rhymes with Fred?

I've actually been dead for almost a month already.

If I were a cartoon character, I'd have Xs over my eyes, and my tongue would be hanging out the side of my mouth. (You're totally picturing it right now, aren't you?)

But here's the thing: Being dead isn't how I thought it would be at all. That's 'cause *technically* I'm a ghost. So is my best friend, Cecily Vanderberg.

T.G. (Thank ghostliness!)

She and I crossed over right around the same time, and

now we live together in our dorm, Jane Austen Cottage, and we go to Limbo Central Middle School.

Weirdly, a month feels both super long and super short at the same time. I guess that's because even though everything is still pretty new for us, SO much has happened already. Like, so much. Cecily and I are totally kicking butt here.

Killing it. (Pun intended!)

First we won the Ghostcoming dance-a-thon, then we started our very own dance club (the Limbos), then I discovered I have an awesome ghostly photography superpower, and then we—

"Lucy?! *Hello?* Limbo to Lou?" I hear a voice call out across the lunch table.

That's me: Lucy. And Lou. Well, Lou's my nickname.

"Oh, uh, yeah, sorry," I say. "I was just—"

"Lost in a trance?" Oliver Rennert says. He's one of our closest friends, even though we've only known him, like, a week. He's also my VP of the Limbos. Oh, yeah, and his older brother, Miles (handsome, brooding, musician-type), is kind of into me, I think? Maybe. I'm not exactly sure. Stay tuned for confirmation on that . . .

"I'm not lost," I say, smiling. "I'm right here. What's up?"

"Did you NOT hear what Briana and Chloe just said?" Oliver asks me, with an appalled look on his face.

"If I say no, are you going to yell at me?"

"We really need to do something about those inner monologues of yours," he jokes. "But *speaking* of monologues, Briana and Chloe are in first-period English together, and Ms. Barnard announced that she's starting her Shakespeare unit today!"

"Okay . . . and?"

"Wait a minute—do you not know about the Shakespeare unit? How can you not know about the Shakespeare unit?!" Oliver asks, incredulous.

Cecily and I just shrug.

Like I said, we're new here, so we're still learning how Limbo works. Limbo the afterlife *and* Limbo the school. Oliver is our age, but he's been here longer. So have a lot of our friends, which means they know way more about, well, everything, than we do. With normal subjects like English and math, we're right on schedule. But with ghost subjects, like Famous Apparitions or Beginner's Telekinesis, we have to start from the beginning. And when I say beginning? I mean BE-GIN-NING.

Once-upon-a-time-before-I-learned-how-to-walk *beginning*.

Even though I had perfected walking by the age of two down in the World of the Living, new ghosts can't walk—they can only float. When I first got here, I was completely see-through and I couldn't physically touch anything because I didn't know how to manipulate energy yet. I literally couldn't even sit down without falling through the chair.

Mortified, table for one?

Things are much better now, though.

"*Everyone* knows about the Shakespeare unit," Briana Clark continues, boinging one of her espresso-colored curls. "It's, like, the coolest assignment we'll ever get in school."

"Okay, so what is it, exactly?" I ask.

"Each year, Ms. Barnard combines all of her English I sections and has them perform one of Shakespeare's plays for the whole school," Briana explains.

"I love Shakespeare," Cecily remarks. "His plays are so romantic!"

"You mean the ones that *aren't* about tragic deaths," I say.

"Even the tragedies always have a love story," Cecily replies. "Love AND death together? That's, like, Limbo in a nutshell."

"Well, the play we're doing is a comedy," Chloe adds. "So no dead people. I mean, except us."

"*And* Ms. Barnard is holding auditions this afternoon!" Oliver cries.

"How do you know that already?" I ask. "We don't have English till next period."

"I'm ahead of my time. Here," he says, passing us the assignment that Ms. Barnard handed out to her first-period English class.

"Oh, *Twelfth Night*! This is so cool!" Cecily says. "I've never been in a play before."

"I'm trying out for the leading man, Duke Orsino," Oliver tells me, "and you *have* to try out for Viola. She's the female lead. Can't you just see it? The Prez and VP of the Limbos in the two starring roles . . ."

"I'm in the school musical every spring," Briana offers. "So I'm definitely trying out for Viola."

"You-know-who will probably try out for Viola too," I say, looking toward the end of our table at Georgia Sinclaire:

aka Black Mop Head McScary,

aka Meanest Mean Girl to Ever Haunt the Afterlife,

aka Bane of My Nonexistence,

aka Ex-Girlfriend to—

"Colin!" Georgia calls out across the room, standing up and waving her hand in the air to motion him over.

I immediately spot Colin Reed walking toward our table, lunch tray in hand. Colin, my handsome, Year Two, first-week-at-Limbo ghost tutor, who *also* might be into me as more than a friend but it's impossible to tell because Georgia keeps getting in the way.

Colin nods in Georgia's direction, acknowledging her call, but drops his tray next to me on our side of the table and plops down.

Ha!

Lucy, 1. Georgia, 0.

"Hey," he says, all dreamy-like, brushing his sandy-brown, slightly sideways hair away from his beautifully chiseled face. I catch a glimpse of the silver ring he wears on his middle finger.

You know what's really annoying? When you like a boy and he acts like he likes you back, but then out of nowhere he decides to get back together with his ex-girlfriend, who makes

Dolores Umbridge look like Cinderella's fairy godmother, only to dump her *again* and reappear acting all nonchalant like he has no idea why you're three shades of CONFUSED.

Welcome to my afterlife.

"Hey yourself," I say back, trying to sound chill.

"What's everyone freaking out about?" he asks, looking around the table.

"The Shakespeare unit, my liege," I say, dramatically sweeping the back of my hand across my forehead to strike an acting pose.

"Ah, I see, my lady," he replies. "So, how was the rest of your weekend as an honor winner?"

Remember how I'm kind of a pro when it comes to ghost photography? Well, last week I entered a photo exhibit in the Limbo Central Museum of Contemporary Art amateur art show and won an honorable mention.

Ghost powers rock.

"It was very honorable," I say. "Hey, thanks again for nominating me for the show. It was really nice of you."

"It was an awesome show," he says. "I mean, even if you didn't hang any photos of me in it."

"Well, you weren't really all that available for picture-taking," I say, my subtle way of reminding him that he spent the better part of last week following Evil McScary around like a puppy.

"Right," he says, smiling slyly and nodding his head. I see his left dimple appear and I can't help but smile back. "I guess Miles was just more accommodating than I was."

Yikes. Okay . . .

Did I use a photo of Oliver's brother, Miles, in my show exhibit? Yes.

Does that mean I like Miles more than I like Colin? Ask me again later.

Does Colin *think* that's what that means? Most likely.

Magic 8 Ball says? The outcome does NOT look good.

"Well, you did lend me your camera for the week," I say, trying to distract him from the Miles thing. "I found that *very* accommodating."

Colin stays quiet, pushing the food on his plate around with his fork.

"And I'm really glad you came to the show too," I say, to make him feel better. And because it's true. "I was pretty sure

Georgia would never set you free long enough to make an appearance."

"Me too," he says. "Thankfully, I'm going to be free all the time from now on."

Hmm . . . is this breakup actually going to stick?

"So, are you trying out for the play?" I ask, changing the subject.

"I was thinking of going out for Viola," he says with a smirk.

"I hear she spends most of the play dressed as a boy, so it wouldn't even be that far of a stretch for you."

"Could you imagine?" He laughs. "Georgia would hunt me down."

"I think I'm first on that list—you're going to have to get in line."

"Next to you?" he says. "Any day."

My knees feel a little weak, and I can sense my head tilting to the side uncontrollably like I'm falling into a daydream, or possibly into HIS FACE when—

Briiiing! Briiiing!

The first bell for sixth period rings, and lunch is officially over. Oliver, Cecily, and I have English next period. Colin smiles and leaves with a wave, and the three of us head over to Ms. Barnard's classroom.

"So, what's going on with you and Colin?" Cecily asks, nudging me excitedly as we make our way down the hall. "Seems like there are some sparks flying!"

"Don't tell me you're back on *him*," Oliver says, like he's already bored by the conversation even though it just started. "Miles is WAY better."

"I hate to state the obvious here, but you're a little biased, being that you're related to Miles and all," I say. "Besides, I'm not back on anybody. We were just talking."

"I know you, Lou, and I don't think you were just talking," Cecily says. "I think it was more than that. Shakespeare is already working his magic!"

Oliver just rolls his eyes, hooks his left arm into mine and his right arm into Cecily's, and sighs. "'Lord, what fools these mortals be!'"

"Actually, that line's from *A Midsummer Night's Dream*," Cecily corrects him. "Wrong play."

"Wrong *guy*!" Oliver replies, laughing. "Now get thee to class, or it's 'off with your heads!'"

"That's *Alice's Adventures in Wonder—*"

"Don't you dare say it!"

Briiiing! Briiiing!

"Saved by the bell," I say.

Oliver smiles. "Time to storm the castle!"

At four P.M., students from all of Ms. Barnard's English I classes are lined up outside the auditorium to audition for a role in *Twelfth Night*. An hour and a half is NOT enough time to prepare for a play audition if you ask me, but no one did.

"Can we recap the plot quickly one more time?" I ask Cecily and Oliver.

"Okay: Viola and Sebastian are twins," Oliver begins. "They're on a ship when *WHAM!* it gets caught in a storm, and the ship sinks. Viola washes ashore on the kingdom of Illyria. She thinks Sebastian is done-zo."

"Like us!" Cecily chimes in. "So, Viola dresses like a boy to find work in Duke Orsino's household."

"That's me!" Oliver sings.

"You don't actually have the part yet," I remind him.

"Just you wait," he says. "*Anyway* . . . Orsino is obsessed with this Countess Olivia, who couldn't care less about him. Instead, Olivia falls for Viola disguised as a guy. Meanwhile, Viola is actually falling in love with yours truly. Cue one big fat love triangle. Eventually, Sebastian, who's not as dead as Viola thought he was, shows up in Illyria, and since he and his twin sister now both look like dudes, everyone is confused."

"And let me guess, they all live happily ever after?" I ask.

"Precisely," Cecily replies.

"Obviously there's other stuff that happens," Oliver adds.

"Yeah, like there's a funny side plot with Olivia's butler, Malvolio, and her maid, Maria, and some other guys too," Cecily offers.

"But you probably don't need to know that," Oliver chimes in. "Okay, I must leave you two now and go over my lines one more time."

"Good luck!" I call out after him, but he turns around and gives me the Look of Death.

"You NEVER, EVER say that in theater!" he cries out. "You say, 'Break a leg.'"

"Oops. I take it back, then," I reply. "Break a leg!"

But he just exits in a huff. Jeez, actors can be so sensitive!

Cecily and I see Mia Bennett and Trey Abbot, and we

walk over to hang with them. Mia is also one of our closest friends here, and Trey is her boyfriend.

"So, let me get this straight," Jessie Rodriguez says, walking over to us. "In Shakespeare's day, only men could perform plays for the public, so they had to play both girl and guy parts. And that's why Ms. Barnard is casting guys in girls' roles and girls in guys' roles?"

"Well, she's not *definitely* doing that," Mia says. "It's just whoever is the best for the part gets the role. Boy or girl. She does it like this every year. It's more authentic to the time when Shakespeare's plays were first performed."

"I think it's nice that she honors her grandfather's memory like this," Briana says.

"Uhm, what did you just say?" Cecily's eyes pop out of their sockets.

(No, not *really*. Gross.)

"You don't know? Ms. Barnard is actually related to Shakespeare—she's his granddaughter!"

"Okay, Limbo is officially the coolest place ever," I say, jumping up and down with excitement.

"So that's why she takes it so seriously," Mia tells us.

"I don't know . . . I think it's kinda weird," Jessie replies.

"I think it's kinda cool," says Trey.

"I think if a guy gets cast as Viola or Olivia, I'm gonna crawl under a rock and die," whines Cecily.

"At least you've got one part of that game plan covered already," I remind her.

The dead part. Ha. Get it?

"So, what part are you auditioning for?" I ask her.

"Well, at first I thought I'd play it safe and audition for Olivia, since there are, like, a million girls auditioning for Viola. But then I thought, what do I have to lose?"

"So you're auditioning for Viola too, then?"

Cecily and I already kind of went head-to-head last week over cheerleading and dance club, and I DO NOT want that to happen again. Whatever we decide to do here, we've got to have each other's backs.

Afterlifelong friends forever. (And all that.)

"Yes, I'm auditioning for Viola," she says hesitantly.

"Cool," I say. "Me too."

"Neat."

"Break a leg," I tell her, and I mean it from the bottom of my non-beating heart.

"Oh, yeah, break a leg!" she replies genuinely. "And, Lou?"

"Yeah?"

"Whatever happens . . ."

"You don't even have to say it." I give her a hug.

"Phew!"

A few minutes pass in silence while Cecily and I quietly go over lines in our heads.

"Hey, Lou?"

"Yeah?"

"Can we just say it anyway? It'll make me feel better."

"Whatever happens . . . You and me? We'll always be GOOD."

"Good."

"So, how many people are trying out for Viola, anyway?" Mia asks, reappearing by our sides.

"Oh, about a thousand," I reply, smirking.

"Me, Lou, Briana, Georgia, Kelly Fitzpatrick, Sasha Kats, and Allie Kit," Cecily replies. "And that's just the people we know about."

"Whoa."

"I'm surprised you and Trey are trying out at all," I say to Mia. "I figured you'd be quite content to paint up a storm backstage."

"And miss the possibility of seeing Trey in a dress? No way!"

"Ha! Well, there's no guarantee, you know," I remind her.

"Still worth it."

"Heya," a voice comes from behind me. I turn around, and there's Colin with a big smile on his face. "Ready to claim another first-place prize, Lady Viola?"

"Not so fast," I say to him. "There are about twenty other *far* more talented and experienced people auditioning for the role. I think I'm pretty low on the choice list."

"But somehow you always seem to end up on top, don't you?" he says sweetly, like I'm some kind of superhero.

I feel slightly faint, but I pull it together.

T.G.

"Well, the same can be said for you, Mr. Football Star, aka Duke Orsino?"

Just then the door to the auditorium opens and Ms. Barnard steps out with a Tabulator in her hand. The hallway goes silent.

"Hello, my dear students," she says. "Auditions are about to begin. Please pass the Tabulator around and sign your name on the audition call list. Students will be called in alphabetical order. Each student will have approximately ten minutes on stage. You will begin by running through a scene of your choice as the character of your choice. Then you will run through another scene of our choosing, as a character that the casting directors choose for you. Casting will go up by nine A.M. tomorrow. Break a leg, and remember what my good friend, the great actor and director Konstantin Stanislavski, always says: 'There are no small parts, only small actors!'"

Just then Georgia McMonster appears next to Colin.

"Hi, Colin," she says, all fake-sweet and innocent. "I'm *so* nervous! Are you nervous? I'm auditioning for Viola, what about you?"

I slowly start to feel my lunch curdle inside my stomach. This girl has done nothing but sabotage my afterlife since the moment I got here. She's thrown balls through my head (literally!), tried to get me expelled, messed with the Limbos, AND stolen Colin from under my nose like seventy-five times.

"Cool," he replies calmly. "I'm going for Orsino."

Make that soon-to-be seventy-six.

I still can't believe she's trying out for Viola. I mean, I guess I predicted it, but it's still SUPER annoying. Normally I wouldn't get so worked up over something like this. Unless it was a role in a ballet. Did I mention I used to be a pretty serious ballet dancer back in life? Cecily and I danced together. Long story, but Cecily and I used to be more frenemies than friends because we were always going out for the same parts. And there was this one time when I got the lead in a recital, but then I got injured and she took over my part. That definitely did some damage . . .

Anyway, as I was saying, normally I wouldn't care so much about a silly play, but this girl just makes my blood boil.

Well, not really, you know, because I don't actually have blood running through my veins anymore. But she totally would if I did.

My point?

The only way this mean girl is getting the part of Viola is over MY DEAD BODY.

(You know what I mean.)

TWELFTH NIGHT

CASTING LIST

Orsino, Duke of Illyria . . . . Oliver Rennert

Sebastian, brother of Viola . . . . Colin Reed

Antonio, a sea captain. . . . . .Marcus Riley

Valentine . . . . Jessie Rodriguez

Curio . . . . Chloe McAvoy

Sir Toby Belch, uncle of Olivia. . . . . Mia Bennett

Sir Andrew Aguecheek . . . . Trey Abbot

Malvolio, steward to Olivia. . . . . .Lucy Chadwick

Feste, a clown; Olivia's servant . . . . Jonah Abbot

Olivia, a rich countess. . . . . Briana Clark

Viola, in love with the Duke. . . . . .Cecily Vanderberg

Maria, Olivia's maid . . . . .Georgia Sinclaire

A Sea Captain. . . . . Allie Kit

Fabian. . . . . Kelly Fitzpatrick

Chapter Two
All Mixed Up

Okay . . . so, just between us? Even though I thought the whole gender-neutral casting thing was cool, I didn't really expect it to apply to me.

Yikes. Does that sound as stuck-up as I think it does? It does, doesn't it?

Ugh.

It's just . . . *Malvolio*? Really?

Here are some words that have been used to describe my character: Hostile. Dishonest. Snobbish. Resentful. Self-righteous. Gold digger. Egotistic.

Oh, and let's not forget this one: MALE.

"Lou, did you see?" Cecily cheers in my ear. "I got it! I actually got the part!"

I'm so laser-focused on finding my own name on the list that I don't even notice anyone else's!

"You got *Viola*?" I ask, in shock.

"Yes! Can you believe it?"

Say yes, Lucy. SAY YES.

"Yes! Of course I can believe it. I'm sure your audition was incredible!"

"Well, *I* totally can't believe it. I mean, I've never even auditioned for a play before. And Briana's been doing this for, like, years."

"You obviously have a gift."

So far I think I'm doing gangbusters acting happy for her. Wait a minute, I take that back. I'm not acting—I really *am* happy for her. Of course I am! It's just . . . my mind is still processing.

Hold, please!

Brain reboot in progress.

I got cast as a guy. And Cecily got the female lead.

I'm a stuffy, opportunistic manservant, and Cecily is the beautiful, clever lady who everyone adores and falls in love with. It's last year's spring dance recital all over again.

Grrr. I feel like an afterlife loser.

I'm an after*loser*!

And a jealous afterloser at that.

"I'm going to go find Briana," Cecily says, and jets off to locate her co-star, who I now notice is cast as the Countess Olivia.

"Congratulations!" I call after her as she sprints down the hallway.

Just then Mia and Trey make their way over to me.

"Looks like we're going to be spending a lot of time together in the next two weeks," Mia says, smiling. "We're like our own little play within the play."

"Did your wish come true?" I ask her hopefully. "Do we get to see Trey in a dress?"

"I guess you didn't see," she replies. "Sadly, no. At least not on stage."

"But if we ask really, really nicely, there's a chance you'll oblige *off stage*?" I ask Trey, giving him my best puppy-dog request eyes.

"I'll think about it," he answers.

"As far as the play is concerned," Mia says to me, "we're both guys."

"Apparently we plot against you and force you to make a fool out of yourself," Trey adds, shrugging his shoulders. "Sorry."

"Apology not accepted," I reply.

"Being serious for just a second," Mia says hesitantly, "since you didn't really register the whole casting list, I'm guessing you didn't notice the other person we'll be plotting and spending *all* of our time rehearsing with?"

"And who might that be?" I ask.

For some reason, my mind jumps immediately to Colin, which is basically the only way I'll be able to make peace with this whole casting nightmare. I wish I could remember seeing his name on the casting list now, but obviously I haven't really been digesting that information. I can't even remember if I looked, now that I think about it! But if it *is* Colin, why is Mia being so weird about it?

"It's Georgia," she says.

Suddenly I can't feel my feet.

Or my face.

Or anything, really.

"I'm sorry, come again?" I gawp at her, praying I misheard her the first time.

Please say Colin, please say Colin, please say Colin.

"Georgia."

"As in Georgia Torturer-of-My-Afterlife-Who-Makes-Me-Want-to-Pull-Out-My-Hair-on-a-Perfectly-Good-Hair-Day Sinclaire? *That* Georgia?"

"That's the one. Her character and my character get married."

Worst. Dead day. Ever.

"Look on the bright side," Mia says, putting her arm around me.

"What bright side?"

"At least you have us," Trey concludes. "We've got your back."

"Except for the scenes when you plot against me with the worst ghost of all time," I remind him.

"Right, except for those," he agrees.

"OMG!" I hear a loud voice scream, and turn to see Oliver staring at the casting list. "Orsino! I got Orsino!"

"Congrats!" I call out, trying to sound upbeat. He wanted that part so badly he could taste it. Actually, he wanted it so badly *I* could taste it.

I feel a little sorry for Colin—he was vying for the same part—but I'm over-the-clouds happy for Oliver.

Literally over the clouds.

"Okay, *what* happened in your audition, and *how* did you end up being a man?" Colin asks me, almost accusingly.

"I don't know!" I cry out. "I thought it went fine."

"Fine is not good enough," he replies.

"Oh goody," I say dryly. "A helpful tip."

"Well, at least Malvolio is a secondary character," he continues. "That's a good thing. You're not, like, Nobleman Number 4 or something awful like that. No offense, Mark!" he yells over his shoulder. "The bad thing is that we won't be spending any time together during rehearsals because I'm pretty sure our characters don't interact, like, at all."

Could this situation get any worse?!

"Bummer," I say, all droopy.

"Totally. Ooh, there's my leading lady! Cecily! Get over here!" he shouts, running over to her. Clearly it didn't take him long to get past the pain of our soon-to-be separation.

Over it, much?

"It's you and me, girl!" he says, linking his arm through hers. "Come on, we have SO much to talk about."

I watch as the two of them skip down the hall toward our Paranormal Energy class, which we have for the first two periods on Tuesdays and Thursdays.

TOGETHER.

"Uhm, *hello*?" I mutter, not really loud enough for them to hear. "It's my class too! Jeez, I didn't realize I needed to be the lead in the school play in order to be seen with you."

The first bell rings, so I head off in the same direction as my two *supposed* friends-turned-bigheaded-thespians, when I spot Miles Rennert walking down the hallway toward me.

"Hey there," he says, half smiling, pulling his earphones off his head. He's always listening to something cool and indie.

"Hey," I reply.

"Haven't seen you since your show—where you been hiding?"

"Secret cave underground," I say. "You know, the usual."

"You are a strange one," he replies.

I'm not sure if that's a compliment or an insult. In all honesty, it could go either way and still be true.

"Thank you," I finally decide to reply. First off, I'd take strange over boring any day. And second, if I pretend it's a compliment and it isn't, the chances of him correcting me are slim to none.

How awkward would THAT be?

He just smiles. "You are very welcome."

We stand in an odd kind of silence as people buzz this way and that all around us, rushing to their morning classes. I think back to what Trey told me about how Miles usually goes for older girls, and I wonder what it is he sees in me. That's if he sees anything at all, which is still totally unclear. He's staring straight at me now, and I feel a small tickle in my stomach.

But is my stomach tickling because I actually like Miles? Or is it tickling because it appears that Miles—a cute, third-year, sensitive musician who never likes younger girls—*seems* to like *me*?

"So . . ." Miles says after what feels like an afterlifetime of silence. "I'm doing a solo set at this place called Dead Man's Cave on Death Row tonight. Any chance you're free and wanna drop by to hear my new stuff? You could bring your camera and take some stills."

"I didn't know you did shows without the band," I say, partially because it's true and partially because I'm stalling for time. (Did I mention that Miles is in a band called Figure of Speech with a bunch of guys we're friends with?)

"Sometimes I just need to do my own thing, you know," he says.

"Totally," I reply, even though I know I'm supposed to say way more than one word. Like, I'm supposed to actually answer his question.

But I can't.

I'm too confused.

I'm pretty sure Miles just officially asked me out, even though what he technically asked me to do is come hear him play music at some café, which doesn't actually involve us going anywhere or doing anything *together* together. But that still counts, right? Or maybe it doesn't? Maybe he's just inviting me because he wants me to take photos of him, NOT because he wants to go out with me at all, and I'm totally misreading the situation and am about to make a giant fool out of myself.

Just like my stupid character, Malvolio. (Apparently.)

This is what's happening inside my head right now:

AHHHHHHHHHHHHHHHHHHHHHHH!

Since I'm lacking the required social skills to continue the conversation on my end, Miles just keeps talking.

"The guys in the band are cool, but you know . . . they're a bit—"

He pauses here, and I think I know what he's about to say. He's about to say *young*: They're a bit *young*. And I think he knows that *I* know what he's about to say.

You know what's awesome about super-uncomfortable conversations?

NOTHING!

"It's okay," I tell him. "You can say it. They're young. We're young. It's cool."

"It's not . . . I didn't . . . Guys are way worse than girls, you know that. I don't even feel an age difference with you."

He blushes slightly, and I do too. I suddenly start to feel that tickle in my stomach grow in force when—

Briiiing! Briiiing!

"We've got to go," I say. "Listen, I would love to come, but I've got my first *Twelfth Night* rehearsal starting at four, and I have no idea how long it's going to take. Plus, afterward I'll have to go home and get some homework done."

"No worries." He starts walking away. "Another time."

"Definitely. Good luck!" I reply, though his back is already to me.

If there ever is a next time.

Once again, at four P.M., all of Ms. Barnard's students crowd the auditorium for the first official *Twelfth Night* rehearsal. Cecily and I enter the room, and Ms. Barnard is already on stage with a microphone.

"Please make your way up to the stage, take a copy of the script from the pile, and then sit down quickly so we can get started," she trills. "You'll use this copy of the script for the next two weeks. Please *do* bring it with you to every rehearsal, and please *do not* lose or destroy it."

As we make our way toward the stage, Colin appears by my side.

"Congratulations, Cecily!" he says cheerfully.

"Thanks!" she sings, and I can tell she feels super proud of herself.

Then he turns to me. "Sorry you're a dude."

"I'm really okay with it," I reply, wondering if faking it long enough will eventually make it true. "Sorry Oliver beat you for Orsino, though Sebastian's not exactly a second-rate part."

"I'm really okay with it," he echoes, smirking. "But I don't think I can be seen with you anymore."

He's kidding around, obviously, but for some reason I still

feel a sting. Is this what it's going to be like? I mean, the second Oliver and Cecily discovered their rise to stardom, they suddenly barely remembered who I was. And now Colin's making this joke but . . . Okay, here's the thing: Aren't most jokes funny because, you know, they're kind of based in truth? The fact that he's making a comment like that means there's something to this idea that you're only as good as the role you got, and that everyone else knows it. What's that saying—birds of a feather flock together, right? Or in my case, ghosts of a—

"Okay, listen up—we're going to get started!" Ms. Barnard tells us. "I hope you are all happy with your parts. If you aren't, well, that's showbiz! I'm going to start by separating you into groups of characters that share the most scenes. Tonight we're going to focus on summarizing the plot of the story, and you'll be using these groups to help with visualization."

Across the stage, I can see Cecily and Oliver giggling about something as Ms. Barnard groups Trey, Mia, Georgia, Briana, and me together.

A glimpse into the next two weeks of my afterlife.

"Okay, so obviously this is super awkward, because you two have a weird thing," Mia begins, talking to me and

Georgia, "but can we please put the revenge train on hold for two weeks while we have to work together?"

"*I'm* not on a revenge train," I say, calmly. "I'm simply trying to live my afterlife without Georgia sabotaging it constantly."

"*I'm* already over this conversation," Georgia snaps.

That went well.

"Okay, here we go!" Ms. Barnard says. "In the fair kingdom of Illyria, there is a shipwreck. Twins Viola and Sebastian were on board the ship."

As she says this, she pulls Colin and Cecily forward.

"Viola washes up on shore," she continues, moving Cecily over near Oliver, "but Sebastian seems to have perished." She moves Colin away to the other side. "Now, there are two wealthy households in Illyria run by Duke Orsino and Countess Olivia, respectively."

Each time she mentions a character, she pulls them from where they are standing and presents them to the rest of the cast. It's like a game of musical ghosts.

"Orsino is desperately in love with the countess Olivia, who won't give him the time of day. Her brother has just died, so she is in mourning and won't entertain any offers of marriage. Enter Viola, who needs to find work. She disguises herself as a man—looking very much like her brother, Sebastian—to avoid being a woman unprotected and traveling alone in a strange land. She finds employment as a steward to Orsino. Orsino sends Viola to profess his love for Olivia, and once Olivia sees Viola disguised as a man, she falls head over heels for Viola. The more time Viola spends with Orsino, the more in love she falls with him, and here we have a classic love triangle. We see this repeated in contemporary movies all the time."

Briana, Cecily, and Oliver are standing downstage in a triangle formation, beaming at all of us, like the stars that they are.

I immediately hate myself for being jealous.

And I am *jealous*.

I'm jealous that Cecily got the lead, which brings back painful memories of the ballet recital gone wrong. I'm jealous that now Cecily and Oliver are going to be spending hours and hours together bonding while I'm forced to play nice with a ghost who would rather set my hair on fire than throw a kind word my way. I'm jealous of the attention I know they're going to get because that's what happens when you get the lead in the school play, like they are this elite popular clique and I'm no longer worthy.

Jeez, that's WAY too much jealousy.

I wish I had an off switch, but none of my emotions ever seem to turn off that easily. Deep down somewhere, I really am happy for them. They are my friends, after all. Then again, what do I know—maybe jealousy is a totally normal reaction? But it's making me feel totally icky.

And I don't like feeling jealous *or* icky.

"Now, over here, in Countess Olivia's household," Ms. Barnard continues, pulling me forward, "we have a subplot surrounding Olivia's steward, Malvolio, whose ego and desperate desire to climb up the social ranks of society force him to fall prey to a trick, where he is beguiled into believing that his employer, Olivia, is in love with him, and he ends up making a complete fool of himself."

You have GOT to be kidding me.

THE PRINCIPAL RULES OF STAGE ACTING

RULE #1:

Trust yourself
and your instincts.

Chapter Three
Did You Say Something?

"Please settle down, everyone," Ms. Barnard calls out over the buzz of chatter in the auditorium.

It's Wednesday, and we're getting ready to do a table read of the play. I should be excited because this is some pretty cool showbiz-type stuff. I've never been in a play before, unless you count the first grade when I was a tomato in Mr. McGregor's vegetable garden in our very low-budget rendition of *The Tale of Peter Rabbit*, but I don't think that counts, because tomatoes can't talk. Anyway, I *should* be excited, but I'm not. I can already sense things changing between Cecily, Oliver, and me.

And I REALLY don't like it.

"Today we're going to read the play in its entirety," Ms. Barnard continues. "Even though we're reading at the table, please recite your lines in character. One of the first rules of acting is to trust your instincts—what you feel, how you interpret your character, what's going on around you. I can't wait to see what each of you brings to your role!"

The table is U-shaped, and Oliver, Cecily, and Briana are sitting smack-dab in the middle, along with Colin and Ms. Barnard, while the rest of us with speaking parts are filtering in along the sides. I look over at Cecily, and she and Oliver are scribbling little notes to each other while Ms. Barnard talks.

I feel like I'm in an alternate universe or something.

I mean, I am. Obviously. Duh, Limbo. But, like, an *alternate* alternate universe, where Cecily is me and I'm Cecily, which is exactly how I felt after I had to give her my lead in the spring recital—like she was living my life and all I could do was watch.

Last night, she didn't come back to our room with me after dinner. Instead, she met Oliver and they were supposedly going over lines until nine o'clock! That's our curfew on weekdays. You have to be in your room by nine, and it's lights-out by ten.

I even sent a Holomail to Oliver's Tabby (aka ghost cell phone, which new students don't get till we pass our three-month placement exam) earlier that evening to see if he and Cecily wanted to hang out after they were done rehearsing.

No response.

When Cecily walked in the door, I thought I'd finally be able to talk to her about this whole Colin-Miles situation, but she was all, "I'm soooooo exhausted! I can't keep my eyes open for another second," and just passed out.

Maybe I'm overreacting. I mean, she's allowed to be tired, right?

Even though she was too tired to stay awake last night, I thought she'd definitely be all ears during lunch today, but I was wrong. We met up in the cafeteria like always, got our food, and sat down at our table. Today was New York–Style Deli Day, and my mouth watered with memories of the trip my family took to New York City a couple of summers ago. The deli sandwiches in New York are, like, piled sky-high with deliciousness. Just the smell of the smoked meat made me think of my mom and dad, and I laughed to myself, remembering the time my brother, Sammy, and I competed to see who could eat the most deli pickles and then we both ended up getting sick.

Sorry, Mom.

Anyway, I hadn't seen Cecily all morning because we don't have any classes together on Wednesday mornings, and I couldn't wait to go over everything that happened with Miles and hear her take on it, preferably before Colin joined us.

"You fell asleep so quickly last night I didn't even get to tell you about what happened with Miles yesterday," I said, biting into my pastrami sandwich.

Yum.

When I looked up, Cecily was hunched over her script scribbling little notes.

"Hello?"

"Oh, sorry!" she said. "It's just, I want to be prepared for today's table read."

"Uh, you can read, right?" I asked dryly.

She just cocked her head to the side and gave me a look that said, *I refuse to lower myself to your level to actually answer that question.*

"Great," I concluded. "Then you're prepared! Now, onto more juicy subjects, I've been dying to tell you abou—"

"Lou, I'm serious," Cecily continued, cutting me off. "I'm

sorry if I'm being lame, or whatever, but this is a big deal to me. I want to be good at this."

"I know you do," I said, trying to be understanding. "And you will be!"

"Only if I really practice. I'm years behind Briana when it comes to training," she complained. "I don't want Ms. Barnard to suddenly doubt her casting and think she made a mistake by giving me the lead."

"That would *never* happen."

"Not if I use every waking moment to rehearse, it won't," she confirmed, half asking my permission, half apologizing for doing it anyway, whether I liked it or not.

"Right," I said, biting into a pickle and feeling a wave of nausea.

I wasn't sure if it was my muscle memory kicking in at the taste of the pickle, or if it was the foreshadowing of the next week and a half of my afterlife.

Of course, ghosts don't have muscles, so there's that.

That's when Oliver came over and whispered something in Cecily's ear, and the two of them bolted off somewhere together as Oliver screamed, "Sorry, Lou, urgent play stuff!" over his shoulder.

And *that* was my great heart-to-heart with Cecily at lunchtime.

"'If music be the food of love, play on!'" Oliver reads his first line, and I snap back to reality.

If music be the food of love . . . Music. Love. Miles . . . I wonder how his show went last night? Maybe I should have gone? It would have been way more fun than sitting around my room alone waiting for Cecily. I totally get that she wants to be good—no, she wants to be great—I empathize, I really do. But does she honestly think that cutting everything non-play-related out of her life for the next week and a half is the only way that's going to happen?

Suddenly I hear a weird swooshing sound in my head—like a wave of traffic flying by, or the wind echoing from far, far away.

"Did you hear that?" I whisper to Mia, who is sitting next to me.

"Hear what? Oliver?"

"No, that swooshing sound."

"I didn't hear anything."

Okay, that's a little strange. But I must just be hearing things. I mean, I *am* actually hearing things, so that's not exactly comforting, but you know what I mean. It must just be in my head. My head's always been a little weird anyway. At least it sounds pretty quiet right now—

Hooooooooooooooooshlasssssssstahhhhhhhhh.

"Okay you heard *that* one, right?" I ask Mia again, anxiously.

"I honestly don't know what you're talking about. Are you okay?"

"Me? Oh, yeah, I'm fine. I'm great. Never better!"

Mia just stares at me with a concerned furrowed brow.

Well done, Lucy. Very convincing.

Okay, just stay calm. I'm sure it's nothing. It's less than nothing. It's—

Whhhhhhhhhhhhhhhhhhhhhhhhyyyyyyyyyyyyyy?
wooooooooooooooooooshhhhhhhhhhughhhhhhhhh.

Okay, THAT is not nothing. THAT is definitely something. Something mysterious and creepy is happening inside my head—apparently—because no one else seems to be hearing ANYTHING. What if I'm going ghost crazy again? What if this is some next-level supernatural thing that's happening to me and I have absolutely no idea what it is or how to control it?!

My breathing starts to quicken, so I close my eyes and try to concentrate on calming down when—

"Ahhhhhh!" someone yells, and Ms. Barnard shouts, "Lucy, is everything all right?"

I open my eyes and Ms. Barnard is looking right at me. Along with literally everyone else in the auditorium.

All eyes on me.

"Yes, of course, Ms. Barnard. Why?"

"Because your script booklet just flew halfway across the room and nearly sliced off poor Cecily's head."

"Oh my gosh, are you okay?" I cry out to her, mortified.

"Yeah, just a little startled, that's all," she says.

"I'm so sorry. I have no idea what happened."

"Right," Ms. Barnard says, "well, let's just pick up where we left off, shall we?"

Cecily hands my script to Oliver, who passes it along to the person next to him and so on until it makes its way back to me, though I'm a bit terrified to touch it. I can't believe I tried to whack Cecily in the head with it! I thought I was over all of that uncontrollable emotional stuff.

Ugh.

Welcome back, Emotional Girl. Can we at least *try* to play nice with the other kids?

The read picks up again, and I concentrate on drowning everyone out and just focus on my breathing. As long as I don't think of anything, I won't feel anything. And if I can't *feel* anything, I can't do anything crazy, like accidentally weaponize a four-hundred-year-old piece of literature.

Caaaaaaaaaaan'thelieeeeeeeeeevvvvvvvvvvvvahhhhhhhhhh hhhhhstopppppppppaaaaaaawoooooooooooshhhhhhhhhh myyyyyyyyyytimeeeeeeeeeeeeeeooooowwwwwww.

Fantastic. I'm officially certifiable.

The rest of the table read goes by with strange sounds dipping in and out of my head. While everyone reads their lines one by one, I can't tell what's real and what isn't. By the time rehearsal is over, I'm so tired I can barely stand straight.

"Hey, are you all right?" Mia asks me as we exit the auditorium.

"I don't know," I say honestly. "I have a bit of a headache."

"You should go home and lie down," she says. "Do you want me to walk you?"

I look over at Cecily, who is gabbing with Oliver and Briana, and I figure she's probably going to stay back and hang with them to rehearse some more. I'll just have to apologize to her later.

"Sure, that would be really nice," I tell Mia. "Thanks."

She asks if I'd like to take the bus so I can sit, but I'm looking forward to getting some fresh air, so I suggest walking instead.

"Not to make your head hurt any more than it already does, or anything, but how is this whole you-and-Georgia thing going to work?" Mia asks.

"I honestly don't know," I say. "I wish we could call a truce, because this constant feud is not only exhausting, it's getting really old. But that girl just keeps getting under my skin."

"Well, I've got a suggestion," Mia says. "Call it a social experiment, if you will."

"Oh, yeah? What's that?"

"Tomorrow, during rehearsal, why don't you try—just try—being *nice* to her."

"Hilarious."

"I'm actually not joking."

"It's because you two are engaged in the play, isn't it?" I

remark, trying to lighten the mood. "You feel like you have to stand up for your betrothed, huh?"

"If I said yes, would you consider it?"

"But she's the root of all evil!"

"Girl," Mia says, smirking at me. "I love ya, but you're being a drama queen with a capital *D*."

"What about the *q*?"

"What *about* the *q*?"

"Well, is the *q* capitalized too?"

"You're ridiculous."

"Ah, but am I ridiculous with a capital *R*?"

"OMG."

"Okay, fine, I'm sorry! I'll be serious," I vow finally.

"Promise?" she asks.

"Cross my heart and hope to beat!"

"Ha! Look, I know Georgia has put you through a lot—*a lot* a lot—but someone has to be the bigger ghost here. And given everything I know about her, I'm betting on you."

"Aha!" I cry out accusingly.

"Aha what?"

"*Aha* you admit she's a nightmare?"

"I've never not admitted that."

"But . . . I just . . . ugh. Fine."

"Fine, you'll be the bigger ghost and cut her some slack?"

"Fine, I'll *try* to be the bigger ghost. But the first misstep from Crazy McMean Girl and I'm done."

"Done with a capital *D*?" She smirks.

"Capital *Y*, capital *E*, capital *S*."

When I get back to my room, I plop down on my bed and try to close my eyes, hoping to drift into a nice, long nap and quiet everything inside my head. But sleep doesn't come. I can't stop thinking about what happened in rehearsal—all those odd sounds and voices flying in and out of my mind like my brain waves made up some kind of psychic trapeze.

And some of them *did* sound like voices. Voices of people I know. And what if this wasn't just some fluke—what if it happens again? I type *What does it mean if you hear sounds or voices in your head?* into the Tabulator's browser window, and the page floods with answers, all of which include some form of the word *TELEPATHY*.

Whoa.

I rush over to my bookshelf and pull out my Beginner's Telepathy textbook, *Telepathy: A Psychic History*. I start reading, looking for something that can confirm what's happening to me. Most of what we've been studying in class is the history of telepathy through the ages—we don't start on theory till next year, and we don't put theory into practice until our third year at Limbo, and *that's* only for students who have exhibited the ability. According to my teacher, Mr. Nasser, not everyone has the gift; only one in, like, a thousand ghosts have the power, and even then, the levels of what they can and can't do vary.

Also, let's be honest, I haven't exactly been paying as much attention as I should be. Class is just so . . . boring. It's not like Beginner's Telekinesis, where we get to jump right into practicing.

> *Telepathy* comes from the Greek *têle*, which means from
> a distance, and *patheia*, which means feeling, and is one
> of the many extraordinary powers of the Spirit World.
> Telepathy is the rare act of communicating via one's mind
> without the use of one of the five human senses, not to be
> confused with telekinesis, which is the power of moving
> things with one's mind, a far more common skill. All
> ghosts can learn how to manipulate physical matter, but
> only unique ghosts have the capability to break through

mental barriers and manipulate psychological and emotional matter.

In this first year of study, we will uncover some of history's most remarkable displays of this psychic art form that were kept secret from humans for centuries. Let's travel back to ancient Egypt, to 2000 BCE, when . . .

Great, this isn't going to tell me much about what may or may not be going on with me. What I need to do is get my hands on a third-year textbook without anyone finding out or asking me any questions.

Piece o' cake.

You know what would be nice? If my best friend were here with me right now so I could talk about the insanity that's going on in my head. But I don't see that happening anytime soon.

I send Oliver another Holomail, this one addressed to Cecily because I know they're together, apologizing for almost taking her head off today.

All she says back is "It's okay."

At this point, I think I'm going to have to figure out how to manage this thing on my own, because Cecily and Oliver are in their own little world and they clearly don't think I belong in it with them.

I look at the clock and it's just about time for dinner. If this *is* the beginning of some kind of telepathic power, the LAST place I want to be is in the dining room, surrounded by ghosts and all of their thoughts, so I should probably just skip dinner. But then again, what are the chances this is *actually* a power and not just my mind being glitchy, which it's been known to be on multiple occasions—and in that case, if I skip dinner, I'll just be glitchy AND hungry.

Ugh.

I think I'm going to go with option three: pulling the covers over my head like a five-year-old and pretending none of this is happening.

Good plan.

Way to trust your instincts, Lou.

THE PRINCIPAL RULES OF STAGE ACTING

RULE #2:

*Don't rewrite
your character's lines.*

Chapter Four
Unexpected

"'Do you not hear, fellows? Take her away!'"

"Jonah," Ms. Barnard began, "the line is, 'Take away the lady!' not 'Take her away!'"

Ugh.

I've never been so bored in my entire afterlife! Ms. Barnard isn't focusing on our characters at all today, so we're just sitting here in the audience with our scene partners watching Jonah Abbot (Trey's older brother) mess up his lines over and over again like he's got some kind of play-induced amnesia. Mia and Trey are a few rows back, studying for an upcoming Paranormal Energy Level 2 test, so I'm stuck here sitting next to Georgia.

Alone.

Death wish, anyone?

I keep wondering if I'm going to hear more voices—if that's even what they are. At least that would be entertaining compared to this! But it's quieter than a library up in there today.

Coincidence or conspiracy?

"Come," Ms. Barnard says. "Let's take it again from Olivia's last line."

"'Take the fool away,'" Briana says.

"'Do you not hear, fellows? Take her away!'"

"Jonah, we just went over this," says Ms. Barnard.

"But 'Take her away' is easier to remember," Jonah protests.

"Ah, but we're not going to change centuries-old literature simply because saying something different is easier, are we?" Ms. Barnard replies. "Especially because substitutions could easily alter the meaning of the text. The words are written this way for a reason, and your job is to honor them."

"This is torture," Georgia blurts out to me, sitting up from her slumped position. "How many times are we going to have to listen to him get the line wrong?"

I think back to my conversation with Mia yesterday after rehearsal.

Here goes nothing . . .

"I was hoping you would kill me and put me out of my misery," I say to her, smiling the way friends smile when they're sharing a joke—not the sarcastic death-threat kind of way. "It would be the only polite thing to do."

"Tempting," she says, staring at me straight-faced. "If that would only work . . ."

"So, were you bummed when you found out you didn't get Viola?" I ask, determined to make this a civil conversation.

"Why? You want to rub my nose in it?"

"Rub your nose in what?" I say, laughing. "At least you're playing a woman, unlike me."

"True."

I can tell she's being cautious. She doesn't understand why I'm being even remotely friendly to her, and to be quite honest, I'm not exactly sure I get it either. But I promised Mia, so here we are.

"Also," I add in an encouraging voice, "you get to make me look like a fool! That must be pretty nice for you."

Georgia shifts uncomfortably in her seat.

"I'm just messing around," I assure her. "It's true, though, isn't it?"

"Fine, it's true," she says, crossing her arms, as if she's surrendering. "It's a little nice, but it's not like I go home and brew evil potions for you in my cauldron every night."

"Well, that's a relief!"

"Look, I get it, okay?" she says. "I'm not an idiot."

"You get what?"

"I just, I know how it all looks, okay?" At that moment, a faint hint of a not-so-wretched Georgia seems to peek through.

"Oh," I say, carefully. "So it just *looks* like you hate me, but you don't *actually* hate me."

"No I don't *hate* you," she confirms. "Jeez. You're *so* dramatic."

This gets under my skin, and the anger fumes start rising. Is she for real? What is with everyone and that word lately?! First Mia calls me a Drama queen (capital *D*, remember?), now Georgia—*Georgia* of all people—thinks that I'm "so dramatic"? What is wrong with this picture?

SO misunderstood.

Okay, just breathe, Lucy, breathe.

(And NO! That was *absolutely not* the slightest bit dramatic!!!)

I have to calm down, because I can't blow this. Georgia and I are having an actual conversation, and that's literally never happened before.

Not in all the days of my afterlife, which, granted, haven't been that plentiful. But still.

I swallow my anger. It feels lumpy and uncomfortable going down. Like cold oatmeal.

"Dramatic, huh?" I ask smoothly.

"It's just . . ." she begins. "Not *everything* is personal, okay? It might seem that way, but it's not always *that way*. Sometimes people do things, you know, for the greater good, or whatever."

"The greater good?"

"You always make everything too complicated," she says.

"I'll give you that one," I say, because it's true.

"You'll give her what one?" Mia asks, appearing by Georgia's side.

"Never mind," I answer. It's way too hard to explain just now. "I thought you and Trey had studying to do?"

"We do, but I can't concentrate in here. If Jonah says, 'Take her away!' one more time, I'm gonna lose it. Plus, I saw you two talking, and I had to come over and make sure you were playing nice."

"She's like a hall monitor," Georgia says, laughing.

"Ha," I agree. "Tell us, Mia, how does it feel to spend your afterlife teaching others to make the right choices?"

"A little stressful with you two yahoos causing all sorts of trouble."

"Oh, puh-lease!" Georgia cries out. "I remember a time when you caused more than a little trouble yourself." At that, Georgia raises her left eyebrow like she has a juicy story to share.

"Oh, are we going *there*?" Mia retorts.

"Ooh! Where are we going?" I cry out. "Tell me! Tell me!"

"Let's just say our first year at Limbo, Little Miss Hall Monitor broke some rules of her own," Georgia says.

"I need details, like, now!" I squeal.

"Okay, everyone!" Ms. Barnard calls out. "That's all for today's rehearsal—I'll see you back here tomorrow."

"Gosh, will you look at that?" Mia says. "It's time to go. I wish we could continue this truly awesome conversation, but Trey and I have to go study for real."

I give Mia a look. "Of course you do. But you're cool if we keep talking, though, right?" I ask innocently, willing her with my eyes to remember our conversation. After all, she asked me to be nice. I'm simply doing what she asked. "I think we might actually be bonding here, don't you, Georgia?" I add for dramatic effect.

(I was being dramatic on *purpose*.)

I look at Georgia, hoping she'll pick up on my strategy and join me over on the dark side.

That shouldn't be too hard for her. HA!

(Oops. I forgot I'm playing nice now. Scratch that last comment from the record.)

Luckily, Georgia doesn't miss a beat.

"Oh, definitely. This is a rare moment. If we don't seal the foundation of the friendship bond now, we'll just go right back to hating each other. It's, like, scientifically proven."

"Fine," Mia says, accepting her defeat with a smirk. "As you were." And she walks off, leaving the two of us alone again.

"Okay . . ." Georgia says awkwardly. "So what now?"

"Let's get out of here and go do something fun," I answer. "Quick, before either of us change our minds!"

We decide to head over to Death Row to go shopping, and as we walk, Georgia relays the Mia story.

"So, this happened before Mia and Trey were officially dating, but she had already developed this monster crush on him, right? She decided she wanted to tell him how she felt—even though I STRONGLY advised against it. I mean, life is already hard enough for us girls—we don't need to be exposing our innermost thoughts and making ourselves any more vulnerable than we already are. Right?" She pauses and looks at me for affirmation.

"Right. Totally."

I'm starting to see what Mia meant about Georgia and her emotional guard. This girl's got more layers than a seven-layer nacho dip.

Mmmmm. Now I'm hungry.

"Anyway," Georgia continues, "we're sitting in my room and we're debating whether she should tell him she likes him or wait for him to say something first, when she suddenly just throws up her hands, says she's tired of thinking about it, and takes my Tabulator. She pulls up a Holomail and just starts blabbing. We're talking total embarrassment here."

"Really?" I say, shocked. Mia always seems so put together, like nothing could embarrass her or throw her off her game.

"Uh, yeah. She's just gushing about how much she likes him, and she asks him to be her boyfriend, and it's all WAY too much. I begged her not to send it, but she wouldn't listen. She just wanted to get it over with already, and she didn't understand what the big deal was. She said if he didn't like her, she wouldn't really care, but she just wanted to know."

"That sounds like Mia," I say, laughing.

"Yeah." Georgia smiles, and for a second I catch a glimpse of something that looks a little like pride.

But she quickly covers it up.

"Anyway," she continues, "Mia presses send and off it flies. We sit there in total silence for like a minute, when all of a sudden she freaks out and starts yelling at me for letting her send the Holomail! I mean, she's going nuts—'How could you let me do that?' 'He's going to laugh at me!' 'We have to get it back!'—on and on. Like it's all my fault! She comes up with this elaborate plan. We were going to go to his dorm and get him to come down and let us inside. I was supposed to distract him while she snuck up to his room—where girls are SO not allowed—and deleted the Holomail. Totally and completely against Limbo rules."

"No way!" I cry out. "So what happened?"

"We actually pulled off the whole ridiculous plan, and just as we were getting ready to say good night and leave, Trey looked right into Mia's eyes and said, 'By the way, thanks for your Holomail. My answer is yes.'"

"Are you *serious*?" I scream. "I can't believe it!"

"I know, right? He totally got it before we even showed up," Georgia says, smiling. "They've been together ever since."

"Even Shakespeare couldn't have written *that* love story better."

Georgia just laughs, but I can tell her mind is traveling somewhere—probably back to last year when she and Mia were still best friends.

The rest of the afternoon is shockingly enjoyable, and the peanut gallery inside my head is either gone for good or taking an evening snooze, because I don't hear a peep the whole time Georgia and I are together. We walk in and out of a bunch of stores, and we each buy something to commemorate the occasion. Georgia gets instructions to this very cool scarf with gold foil polka dots on it, and I wind up with instructions for a T-shirt that has a picture of a T-rex on it and says, WILL SOMEONE PLEASE SCRATCH MY NOSE?

We vow to wear them to school tomorrow as a kind of fresh start.

Our little secret.

When I get back to my room, Cecily still isn't home yet. But I'm not all that surprised or upset. I've decided I'm not going to take this whole play thing so seriously. Let Cecily and Oliver enjoy their lead roles and have their time together in the spotlight. I'm sure everything will go back to normal when this is over.

Right?

Right.

Besides, today was wild! I never thought I'd get excited about being friends with Georgia, but I have to admit, the idea of not only having a truce but an actual, maybe, kind-of friendship with Georgia is, well, nice. And it never would have happened if it weren't for the play forcing us together, and Cecily and Oliver and me apart. So maybe letting Oliver and Cecily have their bonding time is a good thing, actually. It gives me a chance to make some new friends too.

Maybe this could really be a new start for Georgia and me? I think back to today's rehearsal (trying desperately to drown out Jonah's voice) and remember what Ms. Barnard said about not rewriting our characters' lines—that they were written that way for a reason. Maybe trying to become friends with Georgia is my way of rewriting our lines in real afterlife?

And what could possibly be bad about that?

On Friday morning, when I shut my locker door, Colin is standing right behind it.

"Jeez!" I cry out, clutching my chest. "You scared me."

"You're very easily scared," he says. "So, how's my lord Malvolio doing today?" he asks with a formal bow.

"Good, though I don't think Malvolio is technically a lord. I'm pretty sure he's too low on the class ladder for that title."

"Great," he says, throwing his hands up. "First I scare you, then I embarrass you. I'm really sucking this morning, aren't I?"

"I'm sure you can find a way to make it up to me," I say coyly.

"You don't say? How about I make it up to you on Saturday night at Casper's Arcade?"

"Casper's Arcade?" I repeat.

"I'll let you beat me at foosball."

"You'll *let* me beat you?"

"Or you can beat me at something else," he says, smiling. "It's your choice, really."

"That's very charitable of you," I snark back.

"It's the least I can do. So, what do you say—is it a date?"

"Yes," I reply, a big smile on my face. "You should scare and embarrass me more often."

"I'll work on that."

Just then the first-period bell rings, and we have to part ways.

"See you at lunch," he says, that adorable dimple appearing magically and then darting away just as quickly, like a shooting star.

Or a hermit crab.

Did that actually just happen?!

I think it did. At last I have a real-live, actual date with Colin, something I've been wanting since I arrived here a month ago. Yes, Colin and I have had our ups and downs. And I'm not 100 percent sure I should be interested in him *that* way anymore. Or that I even trust him, honestly, after all the shadiness and back-and-forth with Georgia. But I can't deny, it still feels really nice to be asked out by him—FINALLY.

I got this.

Just then Georgia passes me in the hallway wearing

her brand-new scarf, and I feel little goose bumps climbing up my arms.

Could things at Limbo finally be turning around for me?

Mind blown.

Later, at lunch, I'm walking through the cafeteria toward our table with my tray when I run into Miles.

Not literally. (T.G.)

Miles.

UGH.

I didn't even think of Miles this morning when Colin asked me out! Miles asks me out first and I turn him down. And now Colin asks me to go to the arcade with him and I accept. Does agreeing to go on a date with Colin mean I can't—or don't—like Miles? I mean, let's not get crazy. It's just one date. One date. That doesn't mean anything, right? It's like I said, I don't even know if I like Colin that way anymore. And the only reason I turned Miles down was because it was the first night of rehearsals; otherwise I would have gone.

I wonder if he knows about Colin already!

"Hey," he says.

OMG, he knows. I'm a horrible person. I've ruined everything.

"Hey yourself," I say, trying to act cool, even though I'm completely and totally losing it. "How was your gig the other night?"

"It was all right," he says. "I tried out a new song. The record label was pleased."

"Record label?" I burst out, shocked.

"Kidding."

"Right, sorry. I'm a bit off my game today. Fingers crossed I get it back before my foosball game on Saturday!"

"What?" he asks, confused.

OMG. Did I just say what I think I said?

What is wrong with me? Why oh why did I just say that?!

"What?" I say, mocking confusion. "Did you just say something?"

"No . . . *you* just said something."

"Me? What? No, I don't, I didn't."

"Okay . . ."

"Never mind me," I insist, trying to make the most awkward conversation EVER slightly less awkward. "I've just got low blood sugar right now, so I have no idea what I'm saying."

"Okay, well, you better go eat, then. Good talk," he says.

"Sure, right."

He starts to walk away, and I can sense him mentally drifting further and further from me.

From any potential *us*.

Something inside me panics, and I call out, "I'd really like to hear that new song someday."

He turns around and smiles, then slips his headphones back on and turns away again.

I continue walking over to our table, practically shaking. Middle school is so stressful!

I slump into my seat and gulp down a carton of chocolate milk to help me relax. Chocolate milk makes everything better.

"How about we all have a slumber party tomorrow night?" Georgia says to Mia, Cecily, Chloe, Briana, and me. "We can watch movies and eat junk food—it'll be a blast. I have them all the time with the cheerleading squad, and the girls *love* it."

Georgia is inviting me to a sleepover. At least I think she is. Did Limbo just fall through a wormhole in the universe or something?

"What d'ya say?" Georgia continues. "You in?"

She doesn't say my name, but she's looking right at me.

I feel sixteen ounces of chocolate milk start to slime their way back up my throat. What was I thinking, saying yes to Colin this morning—I didn't even think about the Georgia factor! Georgia and I literally just buried the hatchet last night. We're wearing secret-friend clothing to reaffirm our afterlife "rewrite." This is her olive branch! Of course the one night that Georgia suggests having a sleepover is the night I have my first official date with her EX-BOYFRIEND.

Awesome.

"I wish I could," I say nervously, "but I already have plans."

And I can't tell you what they are or you'll hate me for the rest of my afterlife.

Again.

"How about next weekend?" I suggest.

"I can't come tomorrow either," Cecily jumps in. I'm not sure if she's telling the truth, or if she's just trying to save me. "I've got plans with Marcus."

"No problem," Georgia says, but I can tell she's disappointed.

I sit quietly, trying to hear any sounds or voices that may come darting through my head. Things have been pretty quiet in my mind for the last two days, but if there's ever a time when this supposed telepathy power would come in handy, it's right about now (if that's actually what this is). If only I could hear what Georgia was thinking . . . but if I didn't hear any sounds or voices at all yesterday evening when it was just the two of us, the chances of me hearing any now are slim. I mean, if I had any powers, wouldn't they have revealed themselves then?

I guess it might have been cool to have another ghost power, but honestly? I'm relieved. I've got plenty of other things to deal with without dropping some uncontrollable paranormal psychic gift into the mix. Besides, one ghost in a thousand? Those odds are WAY too big.

After a few minutes of silence, Mia breaks the ice. "Well, I'm free tomorrow," she says. "Maybe we can do something, just the two of us?"

"Sure, that sounds good," Georgia says quietly.

"Cool," Mia says.

"And let's definitely do the sleepover party next weekend," I reaffirm.

"It'll be a fun post-play celebration!" Cecily adds.

"Totally," Briana says.

We start eating, and a silence falls over the table. All I can hear is the hum of people around us talking.

"Hey, cool shirt," Chloe says, motioning to my T-Rex tee.

"Thanks—a friend helped me pick it out," I reply, smiling subtly at Georgia.

She nods back, and I feel a sense of relief rush over me.

I can't believe I'm actually about to say this, but things in Limbo are definitely looking up—and not just because that's the general direction of Limbo.

But you know how it goes. Things for me don't generally look UP for too long. I'm pretty sure there's a downward spiral somewhere in my afterlife's near future.

Some twisty, turn-y, how-can-this-possibly-be-happening, no-light-at-the-end-of-the-tunnel kind of downward spiral just around the corner.

(And no, I'm NOT being dramatic.)

THE
PRINCIPAL RULES
OF STAGE ACTING

RULE #3:

Make your
performance
believable.

Chapter Five
Help Me, Ms. Pac-Man!

"Will you *please* get out of here?" Cecily yells, practically throwing me out the door.

"I'm not ready yet!" I wail.

I feel so much better now that I've decided to stop reading into every single thing Cecily and Oliver do. They're the stars, and I'm totally fine with that, and things with Cecily and me at least seem to have normalized. I apologized like a million times for the whole flying script incident, and she totally forgave me.

Afterlifelong friends forever.

But right now my A.F.F. is being a total P.A.I.N.

"You are forbidden from changing your outfit again. You've already changed it twelve times, and as your best friend, I must protect you from harm's way, even if that means protecting you from yourself. Enough is enough!"

"When did you get so bossy?"

"After costume change number seven."

"Ooh! That was a good one—it was better than this, wasn't it?" I say, contemplating change number thirteen.

"I'm not kidding. If you don't leave here right now, I'm going to call Colin myself and tell him your date is canceled."

"Fine, I'm going, I'm going," I say, grabbing my purse and jean jacket. "Wait, is that the *time*?"

"Hello! Why do you think I've been screaming at you to leave?"

"Okay, okay, I'm out. Have fun with Marcus," I say, one foot out the door.

"Every. Single. Detail!" Cecily squeals, reminding me that's what I owe her upon my arrival home—and not a fraction less.

"I promise!"

I exit the dorm building and find Colin waiting for me on the steps.

"Hey!" I say, surprised. "I thought we were meeting at the arcade?"

"I figured it'd be nicer if we walked over together," he says, smiling.

"Sounds good to me. So, how was your Saturday?" I ask.

"Pretty fun," Colin says. "I slept late, went to the slopes to snowboard a little, and then came back and listened to the band rehearse for a bit."

"You did a lot today!" I reply, trying not to think about Colin and Miles in the same room. "I'm impressed. Who'd you go snowboarding with?"

"Trey and Jessie."

"I really want to learn how to snowboard," I tell him. "It looks so fun."

"Well, you still owe me a surf lesson. I'll trade you a lesson for a lesson."

"Sounds like a win-win."

The arcade is just a short walk from the dorms, near the beginning of Death Row (which spans at least five miles from start to finish), so it doesn't take us long to get there. If I'm being honest, the arcade isn't exactly the most romantic first date I can think of, but then again, neither is Dead Man's Cave. What is with these guys? Hasn't either of them ever seen a romantic comedy?! What happened to flowers and candy and romantic dinners for two on the beach? (That stuff's real, right?) It *is* pretty sweet of him to come pick me up, even though we originally agreed to meet there. Sweet and date-like. I guess we're kind of on the right track.

We enter Casper's Arcade at around 7:15 and it's already pretty full. From the moment we walk in, I can feel my mind opening up like an unlocked door to a long banquet hall. Sounds begin drifting in and out at warp speeds, but they all sound echoey and far away. It's strange how all of a sudden I'm hearing a million things, when for two days it was like a ghost town up there.

No pun intended.

Colin spots a table in the back of the room and we sprint to grab it. Casper's also serves a full diner menu, so we each order a milkshake—strawberry for me, chocolate for him— and commence ghost watching.

HaaaaaaawonderifhelikesmewooooooooooShaaaaaaaawwwwww nextgameSSSSSSSSSSSSSSSShaaaaaaaaaSSSSSSIcantbelieve she'sherewithhimmmmmmmmwoooooooooShhhhhhh.

Whoa. It's not just vague mystery sounds anymore, apparently. I'm getting full words, even phrases. *I can't believe she's here with him.* Who's thinking that? Where are they? Are they talking about me?

75

"Lucy, are you okay?" Colin asks, and I realize I must look like a deer caught in headlights.

I'm darting my head around the room like a rabid animal, looking for the culprit of a potentially mean thought I shouldn't even know about that may or may not be about me.

"Me? Oh, sorry about that," I say, playing it cool. "I'm just taking it all in. I mean, what's a girl supposed to play first? Darts or foosball? Pinball or Ms. Pac-Man? Decisions, decisions."

"You play Ms. Pac-Man?"

"If you're asking whether I can play, yes. If you're asking whether I'm any good, no."

"Ha. I'm more of a Donkey Kong man, myself," Colin says.

"Are you? What's your highest score?"

"Around 300,000."

"Whoa. You're good."

Our drinks arrive, and we both dig in. The milkshake is delish and Colin is looking very adorable, but I'm having trouble concentrating with all of these sounds flitting in and out like an information superhighway. And that one person's voice is really starting to annoy me.

For real.

*Soooooooooooooooolamewhodoesshethinksheisssssssssssss
yesssssssIwonderifhe'llcallniceeeeeeeeeeeeshotowwwwwwww
thathurtIwanttogohommmmmmmmeaaaaaaaaaaahhhhhh.*

But it's not just that voice. It's all of them. I have no idea who is saying what, but this arcade is a regular confessional tonight. I thought what happened at rehearsal the other day was just some weird glitch in my brain waves. I didn't think it was coming back. At least I really hoped it wasn't coming back.

I guess I was wrong. If this *is* some form of telepathy, I'm going to have to learn how to control it. Because this?

Is bananas.

B.A.N.A.N.A.S.

I tell Colin I need to go to the ladies' room, and excuse myself to see if I can hone in on the mean girl with the mean thoughts.

I inch my way through the game-playing crowd, walking slowly as I try to match the thoughts to the face.

I feel like an undercover spy or something.

Just as my eyes are locking in on third-year Kelly Fitzpatrick, cheerleader and Georgia's VP on the squad, I crash into someone.

"Hey, I've been looking all over for you," a voice says.

I look up and see Miles standing in front of me. Miles and his cute, curly hair and his fudge-colored eyes.

"Hey!" I say frantically, out of surprise.

Fudge.

Chocolate.

Milkshake.

Colin.

AHHHHHHHHHHHHHHHHHHHHHHHHHHH!

"Thanks for, uh, for asking me to hang out," he says, a shy smile across his face. "It's an interesting choice of place, I'll give you that—it's not exactly my normal scene, but it's all good. I thought for sure the whole Dead Man's Cave invitation made things weird between us. Glad it didn't."

Uhm . . . WHAT??????????????

I'm so confused. I'm so confused. I'm SOOOOOOO confused.

Me ask him HERE?

"Oh, well, uhm, yeah" is all I can muster.

How is this possible? Me ask him to come here? Me ask him . . . like, on a date? The same night I'm out with

Colin—at the SAME PLACE?! This is not possible. This can't be happening. This has to be a joke or a trick or a—

Wooooooooooossssssomuchfunsoreloserhushhhhhhhhhwhyis shestaringmustfillspacesaysomethingssssshaaaaaaamooooo thaaaaaaaasohgodhowwhyhummmmmmmmm.

"I should warn you," he says, smiling, "I'm a mean Ms. Pac-Man player."

"Is that so?" I say, stalling for time. "Well, why don't you go, uhm, stand in line for the game?" I continue, motioning toward the Ms. Pac-Man in the front corner of the arcade. "I'm just going to go to the bathroom, if you don't mind, and I'll meet you over there."

I dart back to the bathroom without even waiting for Miles to answer me, and I shut myself up in a stall. The voices are quieter in here, but I can still hear them clogging up my brain space, and right now I really need some peace and quiet.

I need to think.

How in Limbo am I ever going to get myself out of THIS mess?

(How in Limbo did I ever get myself into THIS mess?!)

I exit my stall, and harass the first ghost I see with a Tabby, who just happens to be a fourth year. I boldly ask her if I can borrow it, and then proceed to send a Holomail to Marcus, knowing Cecily is with him, begging them to come to the arcade ASAP. I know Mia is hanging with Georgia tonight, so I don't dare disturb her. In the message to Cecily, I tell her exactly what's happening, and I ask her to invite everyone she can think of except Mia. The more people who come, the better chance I have at distracting Colin.

I go back over to the table, and Colin has almost finished his shake.

"There you are," he says. "I was starting to think you ditched me."

"What? Don't be crazy!" I say a little too enthusiastically. "There was a long line in the bathroom."

"Right."

I begin sipping my milkshake, keeping my eyes peeled for Cecily and company.

"So, I bet you can't wait to make me look like a chump, huh?" he says.

I nearly choke on my strawberry shake.

"Uhm, what?" I ask, wiping my mouth. *Does he know?!*

"You know, when you beat me in your game of choice?"

"Oh, that. Actually, I think you should go ahead and warm up with a solo game of Donkey Kong, because I *need* to see this high score of yours."

"But that could take a really long time—let's play something together," he says sweetly.

I feel like crying.

Colin is being so nice, and I just want to relax and have a fun night with him, but I can't because Miles is here, supposedly because I invited him, and now I need to figure out how to be on two dates at once and make them both believe I'm having fun when I'm really having a complete and total mental breakdown.

Easy breezy.

I nurse my shake for another ten minutes, making small talk, stalling for time.

"Hey, guys!" a voice cries as Cecily appears by our side.

I mouth *thank you* to her and hope that Colin doesn't notice.

"Oh, hey, Cece," I say. "What brings you here?"

"Well, we were watching a movie, and this scene came on where the stars go to a diner and order this giant ice cream sundae, and Marcus goes, 'That looks really good,' and I go, 'Yeah, it *really* does,' and before we knew it, we were on our way here," she says, plopping down next to me in the booth.

"Why didn't you go to the Spooky Soda Shoppe?" Colin asks. I can tell he seems slightly suspicious about their arrival.

Cecily's eyes pop out of her head a little.

"See, we also wanted fries," Marcus chimes in, sitting down next to Colin.

"Yeah, sweet *and* salty," Cecily says. "There's no point in getting ice cream without fries. That's the dream team right there."

Cecily flags down the waiter, and Colin gives me an apologetic look, like he's sorry our date has been ruined.

I feel lower than I've ever felt in my whole life. And afterlife.

Not only am I somehow accidentally two-timing Colin tonight with Miles, but the only reason Cecily and Marcus are here is to help me cover up for my supposed two-timing! And to top it all off—as if I could feel any worse about my awful behavior—Colin thinks this is his fault!

My eyes start to well up. For the first time in all of my afterlife, I'm actually physically able to produce tears.

Things must be really, really bad.

"I have to go to the bathroom!" Cecily bursts out. "Lou, come with me!"

She grabs my arm and pulls me up before I have a chance to say anything. I mouth *I'm sorry* to Colin, and follow Cecily toward the back of the room, even though Miles is in the front by the Ms. Pac-Man game and he's already been waiting for me for at least fifteen minutes.

At this point, he probably thinks I fell in the toilet.

"Are you okay?" she cries. "What happened?"

"I have no idea. All I know is Miles just appeared and *thanked* me for inviting him here tonight. *Me* invite *him*? Something fishy is going on—but I don't have time to figure out what, at least not now. Now I need to keep Miles and Colin from seeing each other, and I definitely need to keep each of them from seeing me with the other."

"At least Miles is taken care of for a little while."

"What does that mean?"

"Briana is over there talking to him."

"She is?!" I cry out, louder and more defensively than I expected. "Oh, okay, well, good."

I look past the crowd, and sure enough, there's Briana

talking to Miles. She's playing with her hair in this very girly, flirty kind of way, and I feel an urge to go over there, but instead, I head back over to Colin.

"Okay, it's Donkey Kong time!" I exclaim, smiling. I need to keep him distracted, and playing a game all by himself is my best shot.

"Only if when I'm done, you and I play something together. Deal?"

"Deal."

Luckily, the Donkey Kong machine is close to our table at the back of the room, and it's on the opposite wall facing out, which means that Colin has his back to us while he plays.

T.G.

He starts playing, and I hang out and cheer him on for a bit, my eyes darting back and forth between his game and Miles, all the way at the front of the room. Briana is still there with him, and they both appear to be laughing. He is looking around the arcade occasionally—I assume he's trying to find me—but he doesn't seem too concerned. And why should he be? I mean, Briana is, like, literally perfect. She's one of the smartest ghosts in her year. She's a cheerleader and a Limbo dancer, AND she's one of the leads in the school play. Miles is in very good hands . . .

The white noise of voices inside my head comes into focus all of a sudden, and I realize that there's one voice that's rising above the others, coming in nice and clear: Briana's.

Soooooooooocutewonderwhyhe'sherelovehishairrrrrrrrrthis doesn'tseemlikehiskindofplacewhoaaaaaaaaaIshouldtellhim abouttheleadintheplaywonderifhelikesme.

Overload, much?

"Yes!" Colin cries out. "Did you see that?"

"Totally," I lie. "That was awesome."

I'm a horrible, horrible person.

"I'll be right back, okay?" I say, and dart away before he has a chance to speak.

Cecily and I exchange looks as I pass the table, and I notice that Chloe and Trey have also joined them. She nods as if to say, *I'll watch Colin*, and I head to the front to check in on Miles.

And Briana.

"Hey!" he says, spotting me from afar. "Where have you been?"

"Crazy long line in the bathroom. There's like only one stall working—it's a nightmare!" I say dramatically.

(Dramatically *on purpose*. For the record.)

"I was beginning to worry," he says, smiling, fidgeting with his hands.

"Hey, Briana," I say.

"Hey," she replies. "Miles was just about to show off his mean Ms. Pac-Man skills."

"Oh, yeah? I'm excited to witness those myself," I say. "He told me about them earlier."

"It's okay. I don't have to play this one," Miles says. "We can go do something else—something together."

He's directing this statement at me, and it makes me feel all warm and fuzzy inside. But I can't accept the offer or let it excite me, because right now, distracting him with Ms. Pac-Man is the only way I'm getting out of this evening alive.

I mean dead alive, not alive alive.

"No—I really want to see you kick some Ms. Pac-Man butt," I say. "Seriously. And Briana does too."

"She's got that right," Briana agrees.

Miles gives me a confused look, like he thinks I'm trying to pull one over on him. And he's right.

Help me, Ms. Pac-Man, help me!

After what feels like ten minutes of Briana and me staring directly at him, smiling like robots, Miles finally agrees to play one game. While we're watching him play, I see Cecily jump up from the table. I realize she's heading over to Colin, who is done playing his game and is walking toward the front of the arcade to look for me.

"I'll be right back," I say, and sprint off toward Colin.

"Hey, where ya off to?" I ask, walking up to him and blocking his path.

"I was coming to look for you," Colin says. "You're a tough ghost to pin down tonight."

"Sorry," I say. "I was just exploring."

That's when I hear this:

Whydoesshekeepavoidingmemaybeweshouldleave—heyisthat Milesthat'sweirdwhatifIjustblewmyshot.

"I think we should play some air hockey," I remark. "What do you say?"

He gives me an odd look, but then seems to recalibrate. "I say watch out, because I kill at air hockey."

"What happened to letting me win, huh?"

"You lost your privileges when you started disappearing," he jokes, but there's something real in this accusation.

"I guess I'm on my own," I say with a smile. "May the best ghost win."

I slyly position myself at the end of the table facing the front of the arcade so I can keep one eye on Miles and Briana. We begin playing, and I finally—FINALLY—start having fun. The puck is swirling around the board and soaring through the air, hovering here and there, ghost-style. Colin is far more advanced than I am at telekinesis, but I manage a few impressive moves, especially given the fact that I've only been a ghost all of four weeks! We play until it's 5–2, in favor of Colin, and then call it quits.

I realize that twenty minutes have now gone by since I've even looked in Miles's direction. I glance over just in time to see him heading straight toward us!

I lock eyes with Miles, and suddenly his voice streams into my head.

TheresheiswhatsshedoingoverhereisthatColinwithherwhat's goingon?

I spot a girl with a soda in her hand standing right by Colin and before I can think, I will my mind to grab hold of it.

SPLASH!

"Whoa!" Colin yells as the soda streams all the way down the front of his jeans. "Watch it, will you?" he yells at her.

"I'm sorry," the girl says, though what she's really thinking is:

WhatjusthappenedIdidnotspillthatdrinkonmyownwhodidthattome?

"Oh no!" I say. "You better go to the bathroom and wash that before it stains."

"Lucy, I'm a ghost."

"Okay . . ."

"So I don't need the bathroom. I can just clean it up on my own," he says. "Give me a sec."

He closes his eyes and starts to separate the liquid from the fabric so the drops of soda are floating in midair. Even though this trick is insanely cool and I should be taking notes, I'm freaking out because my plan to get him into the bathroom and away from Miles didn't work, and Miles is a few feet away from us and inching closer with each passing second.

Just then Cecily, Marcus, and Chloe appear by my side. AfterlifeSAVERS.

"I'm going to go get that girl another soda!" I announce loudly, and zoom off, while the three of them drag Colin away to distract him with a game of darts.

I rush over to Miles, who still looks really confused.

"Hey, what's going on?" he asks. "I feel like you've been avoiding me."

"No! I'm sorry, I didn't mean to," I say. "It's just, I'm a little all over the place. Cecily showed up with Marcus and, well, she needed to talk to me about something personal, and I've kind of been trying to do double duty. It's a little harder than I expected. I'm really sorry."

"Oh," Miles says, somewhat allayed, but still cautious.

I am literally the worst ghost who ever died.

All I've done tonight is lie to people I care about, but if I tell either Colin or Miles the truth, they'll be heartbroken. What I need to do is end this night right now before things get even more out of hand.

"Look, I hate to do this, but I think I should shorten the evening and get Cecily home. Would it be okay if I took a rain check?"

"Oh," he says again, this time disappointed. "Yeah, okay."

"I really am sorry," I say again, and that's actually the truth. I really, really am. For so many things.

"I promise I'll make it up to you," I say.

"Sure, whatever," he says, and turns to walk away.

I watch him reach the front door, and see Briana trail out after him.

For the first time all night, I can finally breathe easy and enjoy some time with Colin—but I'm not remotely in the mood. I head back to the corner of the arcade where Colin, Cecily, Marcus, Chloe, and now Trey are playing darts.

"Hey," I say, coming to stand by Colin's side.

"There you are! Seriously, you've disappeared so many times tonight I'm starting to wonder if you really exist," he says.

"I'm really, really sorry," I say. "I haven't been myself, and it's super annoying because I was so looking forward to tonight. But then it all got messed up."

"*I'm* really sorry everyone from school showed up. Next time I'll have to choose a more remote location."

"I'm so on board with that," I say, smiling back.

Next time. If only.

"Listen," I continue, "would you be mad if I wanted to call it a night? I'm not feeling so great."

"Oh no, what's wrong?"

"I don't think that milkshake agreed with me."

"Bummer. You should probably go home and lie down, huh? I'll walk you."

"No, I don't want to tear you away from the game," I say.

I really want Colin to walk me home, but after all the awful things I've done and said tonight, I can't bring myself to accept his offer.

"Are you sure?"

"I'm absolutely sure. In fact, I'd be even more upset if, after everything, I ruined your ability to win this darts game, so you'll actually be doing me a big favor by staying."

"Okay," he finally agrees, "but I'm calling you tomorrow to see how you are."

"I'm counting on it," I say with a smile.

I quietly slip through the crowd and their noisy thoughts without even saying good-bye to Cecily, desperate to get some fresh air and quiet my mind from the ruckus.

That look on Colin's face when I told him not to walk me home is burned into my brain. How did everything get so messed up? Maybe I should have let him walk me home, but agreeing felt wrong somehow.

Like I don't deserve it.

Or maybe I just can't bring myself to allow what could have been the best walk home of my whole afterlife to be tainted by the rest of this dreadful night.

Because maybe, just maybe, a walk home with Colin in the soft, cool breeze of a beautiful night would have led to nervous-but-sweet hand-holding, and maybe that nervous-but-sweet hand-holding would have led to unforgettable first-kissing.

And I don't want my first kiss to happen on a night when I feel so awful.

Didn't I tell you that things couldn't possibly look up for too long? That there'd be a dark, downward spiral just waiting for me right around the corner?

Well, I just slipped and fell face-first down the stairs.

And this fall? Is gonna leave a mark.

THE PRINCIPAL RULES OF STAGE ACTING

RULE #4:

Know your story's
structure inside out.

Chapter Six
Maria Strikes Back

After spending all of Sunday holed up in my room avoiding Colin and Miles like the Black Plague, I'm back at school, bracing myself for the first rehearsal of the week. The play is in five days—actually four days—so everyone is starting to get nervous.

Everyone but me.

The break away from people and all of this play drama even for just one day was really refreshing. And quiet. My brain could finally breathe a little.

Not *breathe*, exactly, but you know what I mean.

Cecily spent all day Sunday with Oliver and Briana rehearsing, but I didn't mind. It's like I said, I'm totally okay with everything now. It's like I've reached a level of Zen.

Ommmmmmmm.

Plus, Cecily came to my rescue on Saturday night like a BOSS—even though it completely ruined her romantic evening with Marcus—so whatever feelings of jealousy I was having about her before this weekend are completely and totally wiped clean.

Lemony fresh.

The school day is pretty uneventful, except that at lunch, I notice Miles sitting with Briana. Talk about total confusion. Does he like her now? I guess I haven't made the best impression lately, and Saturday night was obviously a complete and total disaster, so I don't blame him for losing interest if he had any in the first place. It's just . . . I didn't expect to see him and Briana hit it off. She doesn't strike me as his type. Not that *I'm* his type, exactly, but at least I know who Cake is.

Ugh, that was mean, wasn't it? Forget I said that.

"So, Colin seemed relatively normal at lunch," Cecily bursts out as she appears by my side in the hallway.

It's almost 4:00, so we're heading to the auditorium.

"Yeah, things are okay. I mean, he did call me like a million times yesterday wanting to hang out, but I think I finally convinced him that my 'stomach' issues on Saturday night were the start of me coming down with some kind of virus and that I needed to spend the day resting. He made me reschedule for Tuesday night."

"That's good, right?"

"Yeah, I guess. I don't know." I hesitate. "I wish I could just forget what happened on Saturday night and enjoy being with Colin, but I can't stop thinking about it. And I don't think I'll be able to relax until I know exactly how Miles ended up at the arcade."

"Maybe he just misinterpreted something you did or said to him," Cecily offers.

"How?!" I ask, incredulous.

"I don't know," she says. "It was just a thought."

"Okay . . ." I say, and decide to change the subject. "So, guess who I saw eating lunch together today?"

"Uhm, I don't know, who?"

"Miles and *Briana*."

"Oh. Yeah. They did seem to bond at the arcade."

"Right," I reply, annoyed. I mean, on some level I am glad that Briana was there because her presence did help me distract Miles and keep his feelings from getting hurt, but I really did NOT see this coming.

Like, at all.

Maybe I need my vision checked.

"What's wrong now?" Cecily asks, somewhat surprised. "Aren't you happy? It's not like you wanted to go out with Miles, did you? I mean, you didn't *actually* ask him out for Saturday, right?"

"No!" I cry, but that's the second time she's mentioned the possibility of me accidentally planting the thought in Miles's head, and it's got me doubting myself.

I rack my brain trying to think of any possible way that Cecily could have a point. Suddenly, I remember the mortifying conversation Miles and I had in the cafeteria on Friday during lunch, and I literally wince with flashback embarrassment.

"Wait a minute!" I can feel the guilty look on my face. "I just remembered something. On Friday at lunch, Miles and I were talking, and the conversation was weird because I was nervous about him finding out about Colin, so I said, 'Sorry, I'm a bit off my game today . . .'"

"Okay," she says, "but unless Miles is some undercover FBI detective, I doubt he could get anything out of that."

"Right . . ." I continue. "But *then* I said, 'Fingers crossed I get it back before my foosball game on Saturday.'"

"Oh" is all Cecily says.

But the look on her face tells me everything I need to know.

As we get closer and closer to the stage, I feel the steady stream of bits and pieces of people's thoughts seeping through my head, filling the silence otherwise left by not speaking. It's like my brain is a pasta strainer; the full pieces of pasta are kept out, but the pasta-flavored liquid drains straight on through. I spent a few hours yesterday searching *telepathy* on the Tabulator, and I was able to learn some things, but I can't seem to find anything that can officially confirm whether or not that's *actually* what's happening to me.

Did you know that if you want to know your dog's IQ, there's a simple test you can give her to assess her intelligence? You can throw a blanket over her to see if she can find her way out, or show her a treat and then hide it under a cup to see if she can discover it, and a bunch of other things. Well, there's no IQ test for telepathy. There's a doggie IQ test, but no telepathy test.

Super helpful.

I did uncover some instructions on how to control what you can and can't hear, but I have no clue whether or not what I'm doing is working, and anyway, everything I've read says I'm probably too young and inexperienced to be able to control anything. All in all? I'm making ZERO progress with this completely uncontrolled, highly distracting, and incredibly nosy (and noisy!) superpower.

Well done, me.

Cecily and I climb up the stairs to the stage, and part ways. I spot Mia, Trey, and Georgia in one corner, and I head over to stand by them.

"Okay, everyone," Ms. Barnard calls out. "Let's take it from Act 2, Scene 2; we'll start with Viola's lines after Malvolio has exited. And remember: This is where things start to get very tricky, so it's important to know your structure backward and forward! Otherwise, you'll likely be easily confused. Okay, ready, and . . ."

Cecily begins speaking, and the room goes silent.

And by that I mean the talking stops. *I* can still hear snippets of what people are thinking, but technically the room is quiet.

She'sincredibleahhhhofcourseshegotthepartjustlookathersssss sssswhooooooooshhhhhhhhweallthoughtLucywasthebetter ghostbutlookatCecilygodidIbrushmyteethtodayhushhhhhhhh ahhhhhhhshe'ssoprettyandsweetIhopehecalls.

Ugh.

Okay, I know I said I'm going to bury all of this jealousy over Cecily getting the lead and put the whole ballet recital memory behind me—and I am. But it's one thing to try to drown out your own voice in the back of your head telling you you're not good enough. It's a WHOLE other thing to try to drown out the voices of like a million people who are literally thinking the same exact thing.

The truth? It's mind-boggling that she's never acted a day in her life and yet here she is, the lead in this play, owning this character like it's what she was born to do. Between you and me, I'd have no idea how to command an audience like she does—at least not in a play. A ballet is a different story. I'm much more confident when I'm dancing. At least I *used* to be. But now, seeing Cecily up there, watching her truly *become* Viola, I'm not so sure.

Maybe she's just a better performer than I am.

Period.

Maybe she was the right dancer for the lead in the spring recital all along, and I did everyone a favor when I got injured . . .

"'. . . My master loves her dearly,'" Cecily recites, "'and I, poor monster, fond as much on him. And she, mistaken, seems to dote on me!'"

"Talk about a tangled web," Mia whispers, and I chuckle a little.

I can always count on Mia to lighten the mood and make me laugh. My eyes flit over to Georgia to see if she's laughing too, but she looks away from me. I'm not sure if she does it on purpose, or if it's just a coincidence. Either way I shrug it off.

"Yeah, I bet it's rough getting rejected like that," Trey says. "I mean, not that *I've* ever experienced rejection, you know, because this one practically chased me." He squeezes Mia's arm when he says "this one," in a cute, boyfriend-y kind of way.

"Yeah, yeah," Mia replies, "we *all* know the Holomail story."

I look over at Georgia again and offer up a smile. After all, she's the one who told me the story in the first place. She smiles back, but for some reason it feels a bit, well, forced. Not quite as fake as original Georgia, but somewhere in the middle.

"Awww, man!" Trey pouts. "I *love* telling that story."

"Do you?" Mia asks, in a slightly accusatory manner.

"And exactly how many times have you told that story, out of curiosity?"

"Never. I've never told that story before in my afterlife," Trey answers, mocking fear.

"That's what I thought," Mia said.

"But in all honesty," I say, half trying to save Trey, half just talking, "can you imagine being stuck in a love triangle like this? How heartbreaking. I mean, just think how horrible it must feel to be completely and totally in love with someone who's in love with someone else? Ouch."

Georgia remains quiet, and as I glance over at her, I witness a slight shrug of her shoulders and barely the raise of an eyebrow as she looks down at her hands. What's gotten into her? She was totally normal—well, her new normal—with me during Psychic Ed earlier today. Coach Trellis came into class with a new hair color, and I'm sorry to say it did NOT work for her. Georgia, Chloe, and I looked at one another and completely lost it laughing. I didn't see Georgia at lunch for some reason, but I didn't think anything of it. But now this . . . Maybe she's having second thoughts about us becoming friends and doesn't want to seem too interested in talking? It's true we only spent a few hours together one night last week. It's not like we hung out over the weekend, and we haven't even talked at all since that night. Maybe my saying no to the whole sleepover thing made her second-guess everything?

"So, did you two have fun on Saturday night?" I ask Mia and Georgia, hoping to change the subject and coax Georgia into talking.

"So much fun," Mia answers.

"Just like old times," Georgia chimes in, smiling at Mia. This smile is different. I can't really explain how, but I know that it is.

"We went to the movies and then out to the Spooky Soda Shoppe for dessert afterward," she continues.

The Spooky Soda Shoppe isn't too far from the arcade, and a part of me starts to wonder if there is any way Georgia could have seen anything or anyone she shouldn't have seen on Saturday night. Could this be the cause of her awkward behavior?

Before I can ask any more questions, Ms. Barnard moves on to one of our scenes, and we're forced to get up and get into character.

"Okay, let's begin Act 2, Scene 3!" she calls out.

This is where everything goes downhill for my character, Malvolio. Ironic, isn't it?

Malvolio, aka yours truly, is irritated by Sir Toby Belch, aka Mia, and Sir Andrew Aguecheek, aka Trey, because they're acting like wild hooligans in Lady Olivia's, aka Briana's, house. Malvolio is also annoyed at Olivia's maid, Maria, aka Georgia, because she's not doing anything to help, and my character threatens to have the two guys kicked out if they don't shape up.

Honestly, how annoying can Malvolio be?!

We get into position and prepare to begin. I know I should be focusing on my lines and making my character believable and all that, but I can't stop thinking about Georgia's off-putting attitude. Does it mean something? Something I'm not seeing?

"Lucy?" Ms. Barnard beckons.

Oops. I missed my last line.

In which I completely and totally obliterate Maria, aka Georgia.

Oh goody.

"'. . . If you prized my lady's favor at any thing more than contempt,'" I recite, looking Georgia dead in the face, "'you would not give means for this uncivil rule: She shall know of it, by this hand.'"

Georgia glares back at me, but I can't tell if she's acting or if it's for real.

I exit the scene, and Georgia, Trey, and Mia plot against me.

"'. . . So crammed, as he thinks, with excellencies,'" Georgia begins, "'that it is *her* grounds of faith that all that look on *her* love *her*.'"

Wait a minute . . .

"Georgia, dear," Ms. Barnard says, "Malvolio is male. The line is '*his* grounds of faith that all that look on *him* love *him*.'"

"Oh, right," Georgia says. "I'm sorry."

What was *that*?

Hold up—remember what I said about Malvolio being egotistic? Apparently he's so "crammed" with his own ego that he thinks everyone who meets him loves him? So . . . did Georgia just call *me* Malvolio because she thinks *I'm* like him?! I mean, I know I said that both Colin and Miles might like me, but that's only because they both asked me out! That's a totally normal thing to assume when boys ask you out, isn't it? I'm not, like, some arrogant, self-obsessed fool who thinks *everyone* is in love with me . . .

I suddenly get a weird, nervous feeling down in my gut. Especially since things between us have felt strange all rehearsal. I'm really starting to wonder what's real and what's part of her act.

I watch Georgia carefully as she recites her next few lines, hoping that somehow I'll magically break through her mind and be able to hear what she's really thinking.

"'I can write very like my lady, your niece: on a forgotten matter we can hardly make distinction of our hands . . .'" she announces.

"'Excellent! I smell a device,'" Mia replies.

"'I have't in my nose too,'" Trey agrees.

"'He shall think,'" Mia continues, "'by the letters that thou wilt drop, that they come from my niece, and that she's in love with him.'"

Georgia smiles a sly, mischievous smile. "'My purpose is, indeed, a horse of that color.'"

Just then something in Georgia's eyes hits me so hard it's as if I'm being knocked to the ground. It's like a flash of excitement—or of vengeance, almost. Could be she's just a good actress, but for some reason my gut is telling me that's not it. I wish more than anything I could hear what's going on inside Georgia's head right now. Even a word or two could help me, but I don't hear a peep from her. There's still a low hum of thoughts from everyone around me, but none of those voices belongs to Georgia.

I circle back to what Ms. Barnard said earlier about structure and how we need to know what happens in our scenes backward and forward. Let's review, shall we? Maria, aka Georgia McMystery Girl, orchestrates an enormous trick on Malvolio, aka me.

Georgia plays a trick on *me*.

In the play.

But what if . . . What if she doesn't just trick me in the play—what if she tricked me in real afterlife?! Could she be the missing link that tricked Miles into thinking I invited him to the arcade on Saturday? Is that possible? Is that what I've been seeing in her face, in her weird behavior, all afternoon? Georgia's been known to do some pretty awful things since I met her. On the other hand, I thought we were starting fresh, you know? Rewriting our story. Giving each other a second chance. But what if that was all just a big game to her?

Another trick? A way to get me to open up and drop my guard so she could get me when I least expected it?

Grrr. My head hurts.

It's possible that I'm being completely and totally paranoid. The truth is, I did kind of clue Miles in a teeny-weeny bit during lunch on Friday, and maybe I'm just letting my imagination get the best of me. Then again, maybe I'm completely right about Georgia. Maybe she found out about my date with Colin and decided to ruin it by inviting Miles to make me look like a horrible two-timer?! Then again (again), Georgia actually seemed really sincere when we hung out last week, and maybe she truly wants to be friends, and I'm the one who won't let her reinvent herself because I keep coming up with all these crazy accusations and blaming her for things she most likely had nothing to do with?

But then again (again, again) . . .

This? Is exhausting.

"I don't know how celebrities do this every day of their lives!" Cecily cries out, catapulting herself onto her bed and fanning her legs out like she's making angels in the snow. "I'm pooped."

It's fifteen minutes until curfew and Cecily just got home.

"How was post-rehearsal rehearsal?" I ask, trying to sound upbeat. "You were so great today, by the way. Everyone thought so."

"Really? How do you know?"

Oops. Cecily doesn't know about my powers yet, and I haven't decided whether or not I'm ready to tell her.

"Oh, I just heard people talking. Plus, you should have seen the look on everyone's faces when you were reading your lines. They were in complete awe."

"That's so sweet, Lou!" Cecily gushes, clearly moved by this news.

Not that I blame her. I would be too.

"I've been working so hard," she adds.

"I know," I say. "But look—it's paying off!"

For the first time, I start to hear the voice of Cecily's thoughts in the back of my head.

This could be big for me maybe I'll try out for the spring musical too I wonder if I can sing I hope Lou doesn't feel upset anymore she seems okay though so hopefully everything's fine and she won't send anything else flying at my head.

Oh no! I thought I did a good job keeping my green-with-envy face under wraps—I mean, aside from the script incident. And I also thought we had moved past all of this. But if I'm having trouble moving past the ballet thing, it makes sense that she's having trouble moving past the fact that I clocked her in the head with a play script. Now I feel awful! I guess I really am a bad actress. I mean, I knew I was feeling jealous but didn't think I was acting that way. Still, Cecily knew I was upset about her getting the lead—like, she *really* knew. Should I say something? Maybe I should apologize again?

But before I can say anything, Cecily continues talking.

"Briana was saying that you need to basically forget that anyone's watching you when you're up on stage, and think about a time in your life that relates to whatever your character's going through and draw your emotions from that real-life experience. I think it's really been working for me."

"Totally," I say, still unsure whether or not to bring the jealousy thing up. "It's definitely working—you were great."

"Thanks. So, how are things with you?"

This is my window to move away from the play and tell her about the Georgia stuff, and I take it.

"I'm okay, I guess, but I did have a thought today that I wanted to run by you."

"Oh, yeah, what's that?"

"I think Georgia may have been the one to trick Miles into coming to the arcade."

"What? What makes you say that?" she asks, starting to get ready for bed.

"Well, I thought about it a lot, and it's basically exactly what her character does—Maria tricks Malvolio and makes a fool out of him! Having both Colin and Miles meet me at the arcade on Saturday made a fool out of me too."

"But I thought you and Georgia just made up. And she invited you to her sleepover on Saturday night. Why would she invite you to hang out and then totally sabotage you?"

Jeez Lou I love you and all but this is crazy sure Georgia's done mean things but this would be going way too far not everything is the plot of a movie just wait till Oliver hears this.

Wow. I guess it's good to know what your friends really think of you. And to know that they talk about you behind your back.

Excellent.

"I don't know *why* she does anything she does," I reply stiffly. "She's Georgia."

"Don't you think this whole conspiracy idea is taking things a little too far?"

"Considering everything Georgia has done to me—to us—in the past, no, I actually don't think it's going too far at all," I say.

Cecily stays silent.

"What?" I ask, pushing her to say what's on her mind.

"You told me just today that you could have tipped Miles off yourself at lunch on Friday. You told him you had a foosball game on Saturday—that could only mean that you'd be at the arcade. Maybe he thought you were trying to invite him to join you. Did you say anything else before you parted ways?"

I want to stay angry with Cecily, but once again I get a flashback to the end of my conversation with Miles on Friday.

"Lou, what are you thinking about?" Cecily urges.

I sigh heavily. "Well, he told me he had written a new song, so as we were walking away from each other, I told him I'd really like to hear the new song he wrote someday."

"Huh."

"Huh what?"

"Huh 'someday' sounds an awful lot like 'Saturday,' don't you think?"

"Um . . . maybe," I reply, feeling somewhat defeated. "I don't know. I still think Georgia could have done it. She was acting really strange in rehearsal today. I swear, she looked at me once and I thought her eyes were going to cut me open. And she has the perfect mentor to pull something like this off! She literally did exactly what her character does. She forged a note in my handwriting and invited Miles to the arcade—just like what Maria does to Malvolio!"

"It just all sounds really dramatic," Cecily says, looking at me almost as if she's pitying me!

And there's that word again. *Dramatic.*

"I think . . ." Cecily continues. "I think maybe you're reading a little too much into the play, Lou."

You don't always have to be the center of attention It's my turn Why can't that be okay with you Just admit you made a mistake and got yourself into this mess It's okay
No one is perfect.

Cecily's thoughts cut me, and even though ghosts can't technically bleed, I feel myself go white in the face, as if a gallon of blood was just drained from my body.

"Ri-right," I say finally when I catch my breath, only there's a frog in my throat and I trip over the word trying to push my voice through the blockage. "You're right. I'm probably just letting my imagination get the best of me."

Inside my head the wheels are turning. I'm so confused I could scream.

So many unanswered questions. Schemes. Plots. Not knowing who my true friends are. Is Georgia back to her evil ways, or did I just take her place, accusing people of things they didn't do, left and right? Has this afterlifelong-friends-forever pact between Cecily and me just vanished into thin air? And if it did, is that my fault or hers? Maybe if I hadn't been so jealous, so self-consumed, so *Malvolio*, things wouldn't be so messed up?

And then . . .

After we get into our beds, I hear Cecily Holochatting with Oliver on the Tabulator for like an hour. Every time she laughs, I look over and ask her what they're talking about, and she just says, "Oh, you know. Play stuff."

You know what? I've been trying really hard to be cool about letting them have their secrets and their spotlight and to stop myself from feeling jealous of Cecily about the play and the ballet stuff.

But their behavior? Is just plain rude.

It's enough to make a sane ghost go mad.

(Of course, all the voices rushing in and out of my head suggest I may have never actually been sane in the first place.)

THE PRINCIPAL RULES OF STAGE ACTING

RULE #5:

Listen.
Listen.
Listen.

Chapter Seven
Charmed and Confused

"Lou? Hello, Lou? Are you in there?" Oliver calls out, flashing a jazz hand in front of my face as if I've just blacked out.

Fourth period just ended, and he, Cecily, and I are heading to the cafeteria for lunch.

"Sorry, I spaced out a little," I say as I open my locker and place my books inside.

"Don't you pay any attention during rehearsals?" Oliver asks me. "One of the most important rules of acting is LISTENING."

"I'll keep that in mind for the future," I reply. "But also, we're not acting. We're just being alive. I mean dead. You know what I mean. Anyway, what was the question?"

"The *question* was whether or not I should completely

slick my hair back for the play or leave it carefree and curly?" Oliver asks, obviously annoyed that he has to repeat himself.

"Oh, right," I say. "Isn't that, like, the costume designer's decision?"

"*Please*, as if I'm going to leave something this important up to Lana Polasky. That girl has clearly never even seen hair gel, let alone used it. Her hair is so big she probably has animals living in it."

"Whoa, that's a little harsh, don't you think?"

Oliver gives me a skeptical look. "Is something going on with you that we should know about?" he asks. "You've been acting MUCHO weird this week."

It's jealousy total and complete jealousy. Unbelievable.

"*I'm* acting weird?" I say, shocked.

Great, now Oliver thinks I'm jealous too! And look, okay, I was a little jealous, but now they're taking things too far. I literally can't believe what I'm hearing—both aloud and inside his head. Oliver and Cecily have been secluded in their own little club of two since this whole play thing started, essentially ignoring my existence (or is it nonexistence?) and getting all high-and-mighty because they're the leads, and *I'm* the one being weird? I mean, it's only a school play! It's not like they got picked to be on *So You Think You Can Dance*!

"Yes. You're acting *aloof*," he says matter-of-factly.

"I've sent you like three Holomails in the past week that you guys never answered because you were too busy rehearsing, and *I'm* being aloof?"

"Well, you haven't even asked me once how rehearsals are going."

"I'm in the rehearsals *with* you," I point out. "I know how they're going. We're all in the play together, remember?"

"Yes, but it's different," he says with a smug shrug of his shoulders. "Being the lead is . . . Well, there's more pressure to, you know, perform. Right, Cecily?"

Cecily's eyes start darting around the room, as if she's trying to avoid answering the question. But I know what she's thinking already.

Uh-oh
I hate this

I don't want Lou to be mad at me but it is a little different
I wish she could just be supportive
I'm always supportive of her.

How do things always gets turned back on me?! When Cecily wanted to try out for the cheerleading squad, who was there watching her practice her routine and cheering her on in the stands at the tryouts? ME. Even though Georgia is the captain and was trying to sabotage my dance club. How can Cecily possibly think that I don't support her? That's just . . . WRONG. Didn't I literally just compliment her last night on what a great job she's doing in the play? I'm the one who should be questioning *her* loyalty. I mean, instead of listening to my theory about Georgia and helping me get to the bottom of it, she stands there thinking I'm nuts and trying to convince me that it's all my fault.

GRRRRRRRRRRRRRRRRRRRRRRRRRRRR!

"It is a little different," Cecily finally says, sheepishly.

"Right," I reply, furiously slamming my locker door shut. "Obviously, since I'm just a lowly manservant, I can't possibly understand how much pressure you two are under. I forgot your acting careers are riding on that *Entertainment*

Weekly review. Now, if you'll excuse me, I'm going to get some air."

I storm down the hallway as quickly as I can. If I don't get away from the two of them, Emotional Girl is going to do some serious damage.

The nerve of them! I mean, do they even have any idea what I'm going through with this whole potential telepathy thing? And the fact that there's a very good possibility that someone is plotting against me behind my back? And THEY'VE got pressure?

PUH-LEASE.

As I sprint down the hallway like I'm running in the Olympics, I once again smash right into Miles.

"Ouch!" I yelp, rubbing my left shoulder.

"Whoa, watch out," he says, then looks up. "Oh, it's you. Sorry, are you okay?"

"No, *I'm* sorry," I say back. "It's all my fault. I totally wasn't paying attention."

"Going somewhere in a hurry?"

"Yes, in fact. Very much so. Care to join me?"

I'm not sure what gets into me, but something about

Miles's presence is soothing, and I still feel awful about how things ended on Saturday. I told him I'd make it up to him, didn't I?

"Sure, why not," he replies.

Miles is the embodiment of the word CHILL.

We walk out of the school and into the courtyard where there are some picnic tables and benches, and he starts heading toward one of the tables.

"Actually, do you mind if we just walk for a bit?" I say.

I need to get as far away from this place as possible. For my sanity.

Or lack thereof.

"No problem," he says with a smile.

"So, how was your set at Dead Man's Cave the other day? I didn't even get to ask you."

Actually you did ask me the other day at lunch
Wonder what's going on
Something doesn't seem right.

"Oh, right, I'm sorry," I say instinctively. "You're right, I did ask you. You made a joke about a record label."

"What?" He looks at me, confused. "What do you mean, 'I'm right'? I didn't say anything."

Oh, for the love of Limbo, not *again*. What's wrong with me? Why can't I keep anything inside my head straight?!

"Uhm, I meant 'you're right' as a figure of speech," I stutter, "not that you—not that you actually said something. I just remembered that I did ask you. I'm sorry, my brain's a bit jumbled."

"Okay . . ." he replies cautiously.

Then there's just silence.

I feel weird. I want to say something, but I don't know what. Maybe inviting him to walk with me was a bad idea? That seems to be all I'm good for these days . . .

"So, Saturday night was enjoyable," he remarks, filling the silence, "even if you were a bit all over the place."

"Yeah? I mean, yeah, it was nice. I'm sorry, though, that things got all messed up. But it seems like you and Briana hit it off."

Ugh. I shouldn't have said that. I *really* shouldn't have said that.

Ouch, low blow.

"She's cool," he says. "I didn't think I was going there to hang out with her, though."

"I know," I reply.

I SO deserved that.

"How are things with Cecily?" he continues, changing the subject. "You said something was wrong with her on Saturday night?"

I wonder if she's actually going to tell me the truth or if she's going to keep lying to me.

Hmmmm I guess we'll see soon enough.

Great. Miles knows I was lying!

I HATE afterlife.

Just then he looks at me with a strange expression, like he's just seen a . . . well . . . a ghost. All the color drains from his face.

No pun intended.

"Are you okay?" I ask, concerned.

"Yeah, I'm fine," he says, though he's not super convincing.

Is this really happenincrrrrrrrrrrrrrrrrrrrrrrrr
eeeeeeeeeeeeeeeeeekkkkkkkkkkkkkkkkkkk—

All of a sudden, his thoughts blank out, like someone just cut the electricity and the music stopped. Something weird is happening, and I have no idea what it is.

"So, you were just going to tell me about Cecily?" he asks, staring at me eagerly.

Okay, this is my moment: to tell or not to tell. He thinks I was lying about Cecily, and he's right, so now's my chance to come clean. Then again, if I tell him I didn't actually invite him to the arcade after all—that it was all some kind of mix-up—it will crush him, and I don't want to crush him. I like him, I think.

"Oh, yeah," I say, finally. "She's okay, thanks for asking. Just needed some friend time to sort through something, is all."

Wow she didn't even crrrrrrrrrrreeeeeeeeekkkkkkkkk—

Again? Why's it cutting out like that? Am I malfunctioning or something? Maybe I don't have any powers after all and it's all been in my head? Or maybe it's just fading?

I'm so confused.

I wish I could to talk to someone about this, but I can't tell anyone. Not yet. Things with Cecily and Oliver are super weird, and it's hard to get Mia alone at rehearsal because

Georgia's always there, and even though we're supposed to be playing nice with each other, I don't actually think I can trust her.

I wish I could ask Miles, but he probably hates me right now.

I can't say that I blame him. He's so nice and cool and cute, and I'm a walking mess.

"I'm glad she's okay," Miles says, smiling at me. "And thanks for the walk; you can hit me up for one of these anytime."

"Cool."

"Cool."

Okay, I guess Miles doesn't hate me . . .

Cool.

At six thirty that night, I head over to Colin's dorm for our rescheduled—er, second—date. I'm excited to finally spend some time alone with Colin, even though I haven't had five minutes of free brain space to actually think about it. And yet . . . I can't get my walk with Miles today out of my head. Aside from the weird mind-reading stuff, it was so . . . relaxing.

Sure, Miles is kind of quiet, but I like that. I can think when I'm around him, and I don't feel like I have to talk all the time. We can just be, and it's okay. And there's no drama. No ex-girlfriends—or at least not ones that want to make me die a slow and painful re-death for liking him.

Well, not that I've met yet.

Colin greets me at the door, and we head up to one of the communal rooms to watch a movie. This time we're watching one of *my* favorites: *The Princess Bride*.

I know it sounds super girly but it's SO not. It's full of adventure and fantasy, and it's HILARIOUS. It'll be really nice to shut down my brain and enjoy something I love with someone I like a whole lot.

I think.

We start up the movie, and Colin and I are sitting on the couch next to each other, almost touching. I've never sat this close to a boy before. What if I'm doing it wrong? Wait a minute—that's crazy, right? You can't sit the wrong way. Can you? I mean, it's not like I'm sitting backward and wondering why I can't see the Holoscreen?

Ha. I'm not THAT much of a mess.

I can't believe this is finally happening
I'm so happy I hope she's having fun
How did I waste so much time on Georgia
I'm so dumb.

Okay, I guess I'm not sitting the wrong way after all. Also, apparently my powers aren't malfunctioning either, because I can hear Colin's thoughts just fine, clear airwaves all the way. It must have just been a Miles thing . . . I'll have to do some serious research tomorrow to figure this thing out once and for all. What happened with Miles was straight-up odd.

Anyway, back to Colin . . . It's strange to finally know for sure how Colin is feeling about me after so much time spent guessing. But I suppose this settles it.

Colin likes me.

Colin Reed, aka super cute, Year Two, ex-tutor, perfect-in-every-way ghost boy, really likes me. And bonus! He regrets all the time he "wasted" on Georgia.

That should make me feel good, right? I mean, if I knew that a week or two ago, I literally would have jumped for joy. But for some reason, now it's making me feel a little weird, even sad for Georgia. I have to get to the bottom of whether or not she's the one who tricked Miles. Because if she did? I CANNOT feel bad for her under any circumstances. But if she didn't . . .

"This movie is great!" Colin says, snapping me out of my inner monologue.

"I know, isn't it?" I reply happily. "It was my brother's and my favorite movie growing up. I'm pretty sure my parents, like, went to see this in the theater on one of their dates before they were married, so they were always talking about it when we were little. I remember the first time we watched it, and we were so excited to finally be seeing this movie they talked about ALL THE TIME. After that, my father would walk around the house randomly shouting, 'My name is Inigo Montoya. You killed my father. Prepare to die!'"

"So there's acting in your blood?" Colin jokes.

"Clearly. How else do you think I landed such a good part in the play?"

Colin just looks at me with a huge smile on his face. "Do you mind if we pause the movie for a sec?"

"Nope, that's fine. What's up?"

"Well," he says, shifting a bit to dig into one of his pockets. "Since you brought up the play, I wanted to give you this. It's kind of like a good-luck charm."

He pulls a little drawstring velvet bag out of his pocket and hands it to me.

"Really? This is so sweet, Colin. Thank you," I say, taking the gift from him. "But it's totally not necessary."

"And isn't that the whole fun of giving gifts in the first place?" he jokes.

I open the bag and pull out a beautiful silver key necklace with a ruby-colored stone in the middle.

"Colin, this is beautiful!" I say, stunned.

"Do you really like it? It took me three days to make."

"It's amazing," I tell him, unhooking the clasp and putting it around my neck. "I love it. Thank you."

"You're welcome. So . . . should we keep watching?"

"Definitely," I say.

We turn back toward the screen, and as we settle in, Colin takes hold of my hand.

Phew that was nerve racking
But she seemed to like it

I think that's a good sign
Now I can finally relax.

Mind blown. Again. Like, A LOT.

I just got a necklace from a boy. Me. Lucy Lou Chadwick got a necklace from Colin Reed. And what now? Does it symbolize something? Is that code for us being, like, a thing? I mean, he called it a good-luck charm, so maybe that's all it is? Or maybe not? Either way, this is by far the most (and only) romantic thing that's ever happened to me in all of my afterlife.

I can't wait to tell Cecily!!

That is, if she's still talking to me after I exploded all over her and Oliver today for reading thoughts in their heads I'm not supposed to know about.

Okay, so at least one unanswered question has finally been answered: Does Colin officially want to date me? YES.

Now where's my Magic 8 Ball to answer the rest?!

Do I like Colin more than I like Miles? ALL SIGNS POINT TO YES . . .

Did Georgia plot against me to trick Miles? ASK AGAIN LATER.

Will Cecily and Oliver forgive me? CANNOT PREDICT NOW.

Grrrr. Just once I'd like to be happy about one thing without having to worry about a million other things at the same time. Is that really too much to ask?!

Why does it always feel like my afterlife is an after*mess*, and I'm the one stuck holding the mop?

Attention: Clean up in aisle 3!

THE
PRINCIPAL RULES
OF STAGE ACTING

RULE #6:

Eat your ego.

Chapter Eight
The Wall

YES! This? Is exactly what I need!

Are YOU a Telepath?, *Breaking Through the Telepathic Wall*, *Telepathic Beginnings: The Jenny Lee Story*, *Telepathy and Me: A Memoir*, *Telepathy through the Ages*, *Telepathy: A Psychic History*, *Troubleshooting Telepathy*.

I slipped out of our room early this morning to see if I could finally get some assistance in the telepathy department by storming the Limbo Central Middle School library.

I'm finding so much good information here it's crazy. I can't believe I didn't come here earlier!

What. Was. I. Thinking.

Anyway, here are several things I've concluded after scouring the pages of *Troubleshooting Telepathy* and *Are YOU a Telepath?*

1. I am, in fact, a telepath. (Yay?)
2. Apparently, I'm "blossoming" before my time. (I guess this makes sense, because let's face it, Emotional Girl has made me pretty powerful in other ghostly ways. Why should this be any different?)

And . . .

3. I need MAJOR help figuring out how to get this under control.

According to my research, being a telepath is actually pretty serious. I'm hearing things I'm not supposed to be hearing, which means I know things I'm not supposed to know. And what I do with that information? Well, that is the question . . .

> There are four main ways in which telepathy can be used:
> (1) Mind Imprinting, the process of imprinting a thought,
> feeling, or image into someone else's mind; (2) Mind
> Control, the act of controlling someone's actions or
> feelings; (3) Mind-to-Mind Communication, connecting to
> someone else's mind and exchanging connected thoughts
> with that ghost as if you are having a conversation; and (4)

Mind Reading, the process of listening, or "reading," someone else's thoughts.

Uhm . . . mind control! Mind-to-mind communication!! WHAT?!

I can't even imagine all the INSANE things I could do with these abilities, that is, if I can nurture them. Then again, I also need to be cautious.

According to these texts, "ethically" it's my responsibility to act appropriately and be considerate of other people's privacy. Just because I have this ability doesn't mean I have people's *permission* to use it on them, which I never really thought about until now. But it's SO true.

And apparently? Without permission, I've been essentially stealing information from people's heads.

LIKE A SPY.

(Which, on the one hand, I *have* to admit is totally awesome.)

But, on the other hand, this is where things get tricky. I mean, it's not as if getting permission is either (a) easy, (b) normal, or (c) logical, since the whole point of reading someone's mind is to know thoughts they've opted not to share with anyone. I mean, how awkward is it to go up to someone and be like, "Uhm, excuse me, but you won't be offended if I read all the thoughts going through your mind that you purposely decided not to say out loud while we have this conversation, will you? Great!"

As if *that* would ever happen.

Still, there are rules about using telepathic powers on people. Apparently, you're supposed to register yourself as a telepath with the TSOA (Telepathic Society of Afterlife) *and* tell people when you meet them so they have the option of "shielding" themselves, which I'll get to in a minute. But that isn't required until after a ghost graduates and enters the real world of Limbo. Since we're still in school, the rules are different—but I'm pretty sure Limbo Central has its own rules about telepaths.

Limbo Central has rules about EVERYTHING.

Anyway, according to Dr. J. B. Rhine, people have the ability to learn how to block their psyches from "unwanted mental intruders."

That's me.

Hence the reason we're supposed to register ourselves.

Breaking into someone's mind is kind of like hacking into

his or her computer. Some ghosts' passwords are stronger than others. This barrier is apparently called the Wall. Ghosts can have Walls of any strength, or they can have none at all. The Wall takes power and control to build and maintain, so you can't just create it and then forget about it; otherwise it can easily be broken down.

Now, according to Dr. Rhine, if someone has a Wall up, and it's relatively well constructed, a telepath would have to work really hard to get through it, and in some cases wouldn't be able to break through at all.

This immediately makes me think of my lunchtime walk with Miles . . . He *did* look at me awfully funny a few times, as if he'd just been let in on some kind of secret. I mean, I did kind of give myself away—again—when I reacted to his thoughts about the Dead Man's Cave thing.

So dumb.

But he looked at me like I had nine heads.

(Which I KNOW I didn't have.)

AND it was literally right after I saw that expression on his face that I suddenly couldn't hear his thoughts anymore. They just cut out. Like someone pulled the plug.

Or put up a Wall.

Whoa. What if Miles knew I was reading his thoughts? He *is* a third year. He could totally have figured it out and then tried to block me from getting in!

OMG, what if he's a telepath too?

Wow. This Wall thing has completely blown my mind. And what about Georgia?!

That girl's got more walls up than a maze! She probably has a Wall of steel, and it's not about to be broken down by spending two hours with me and buying secret friendship presents. Now it makes all kinds of sense why I couldn't hear any of her thoughts those times I was near her—including the evening we spent alone together—yet I could hear so many other people.

If she somehow managed to find out about my date with Colin, even if she was thinking of letting me in before, she definitely changed her mind. Maybe that's why she was being weird at rehearsal that day? Except the whole date disaster happened before that, so maybe I'm getting ahead of myself.

Either way, first step? To figure out how to break through Georgia's Wall and see once and for all if she's the one who tricked Miles.

I got this.

Lunch is finally here, and even though I spent last period with Georgia, I didn't make any headway breaking through the Wall. Coach Trellis showed up to P.E. with yet another hair color, and once again Chloe, Georgia, and I all looked at one another and died laughing.

No pun intended. Times two.

Ugh. I need to get inside her head somehow. Maybe with more people around at lunch she'll be distracted enough to let her guard down.

I strategically place myself across the table from her and set my tray down. Apparently, seeing people's eyes is helpful when trying to break through the Wall.

"So, Georgia," I say, biting into my chicken burrito and staring into her eyes, "how are things going with Maria?"

"As in Maria, my part in the play?" she asks, a bit confused.

"Yeah. Do you feel like you've really embraced your character?"

I think I'll go sit with Miles today
Unless that's too much
I mean we did just sit together two days ago

But I really really want to see him
I think I'm just gonna do it and hope for the best.

Suddenly, Briana stands up with her tray and leaves the table. I know *exactly* where she's going.

Whatever. I need to concentrate on Georgia now, not on Miles and Briana.

Not that there even is a Miles and Briana.

At least not yet.

"I've embraced her as much as I can embrace some maid from a thousand years ago," Georgia replies, shrugging. "Have you embraced *Malvolio*?"

"No!" I reply more harshly than I expected. "And I never shall!" I add, trying to play it off in some dramatic, Shakespearean style. "He's awful. No wonder you hate me so much. I mean, no wonder your *character* hates *mine* so much. It's like, if I were you, I wouldn't think twice about wanting to make a fool out of me!"

I stare at Georgia, trying to catch anything—a flicker of her eyes, a flash of doubt, some glimpse into the inner workings of her brain.

What do I get?

Zilch.

Zero.

Nada.

"It's just a play," she says, unmoved. "That stuff doesn't actually happen in real life."

Is she saying that because she had nothing to do with the Miles thing? Or precisely because she *did* have something to do with it and is trying to throw me off track?

"I guess. At least, I hope not. I mean, that's a pretty cruel thing to do to someone."

Georgia shifts uncomfortably in her seat, and it seems like a sign. She did the same thing when I first started talking to her that day in rehearsal, before we became "friends." If I could only hear some proof . . .

I quickly glance over to where Miles and Briana are sitting, and catch a glimpse of them laughing. What could they possibly be laughing at all the time? I know it's none of my business, and it's totally not my place to care who Miles eats his lunch with, especially since things have been so good between Colin and me. Ever since our amazing date on Tuesday, we've been talking on the Tabulator every night, which I know is only two nights, but it's something. We never Holochatted before. Plus, I haven't taken off the necklace he gave me.

It's still a little unclear whether or not we're an actual THING. I mean, we haven't even kissed yet, so that might be part of the confusion. But I'm sure we'll sort it out eventually.

My point? I really shouldn't be concerned with Miles at all—and I KNOW that—but I just feel so confused. One minute he's taking walks with me and telling me he's open to hanging out anytime, not to mention asking me out on dates, and the next he's eating lunch with Briana every day.

Fine, not every day. Two days.

But still.

Whatever, back to the task at hand.

"Don't you agree?" I turn back to Georgia and continue prodding.

There's a silence while Georgia picks at her food, then looks up and realizes I'm directing this question at her.

"Oh, me? Again? Don't I agree about what?"

"Agree that what Maria does in the play is a really cruel thing to do?"

"Sure, yeah," she says, dropping her spoon. "Anyway, I just remembered, I have to go talk to Coach about something squad-related. See you all later."

Then Georgia gets up and leaves.

Great! A lot of good that did.

"What's with the third degree?" Cecily whispers to me as Georgia walks away.

"What do you mean?" I ask.

"I mean, why are you pressing Georgia about Maria and the whole trick thing? I thought you dropped that?"

"No, *you* dropped it because you don't believe me. *I* didn't drop it. I still think it's very likely that she did it."

"Lou, I really think you've let the play go to your head."

"*I've* let the play go to *my* head?" I repeat, in shock.

"Yes. Briana was telling me and Oliver that when you live and breathe something like a theater production, it's really easy to get so caught up in it that you can sometimes confuse the production with reality."

"Is that so?" I say, wondering how it's possible she doesn't see the complete and total irony here.

If anyone is too caught up in the play to not see reality, it's Cecily and Oliver!

"Yeah," she continues, unfazed. "That's why there are so many romances between co-stars on movie sets and stuff. It's hard to tell the difference between who you really are and the character you play, sometimes."

"So you're telling me I'm acting like Malvolio?"

"No, I'm saying that you're getting Georgia the person mixed up with her character, and you're turning the play into some kind of real-life drama."

I know exactly why Cecily is saying these things. She thinks I'm out to be the center of attention—which is like the COMPLETE opposite of what I like to be. But I heard her think it just the other day, and it's what she's still thinking right now. She can't see that this Georgia thing could be real because she's afraid it will take the focus off of her and, in her mind, this is HER moment.

I'm so frustrated I could scream. Again.

But I won't.

You know why? Because unlike SOME people, I'm going to take a little page out of Ms. Barnard's book and be the bigger ghost. Apparently when you act, you're supposed to eat your ego, because it's not about one person—one part—it's about what's best for the production as a whole.

And right now? This whole will be a WHOLE lot better off if I change the subject. Like now.

This conversation?

Is O.V.E.R.

And . . . scene!

THE PRINCIPAL RULES OF STAGE ACTING

RULE #7:

Always raise the stakes.

Chapter Nine
Proof

Friday is finally here. The BIG day. The stakes are high, and the energy in the halls is supercharged. Everyone in the play is anxiously walking around like zombies.

Or very easily frightened stray cats.

Even I have to admit I'm a bit nervous. My mind has been all over the place during these past two weeks, but now that it's Friday and I'm about to go on stage in front of like three hundred people, it's starting to actually hit me.

Yikes.

Plus, we don't even start getting ready until after lunch, so we have to get through a full morning of classes first.

Distracted, much?

T.G. it's already third period. Chloe, Georgia, and I are

heading over to the gym for P.E., when I spot Colin rounding the corner, walking toward us.

"Hey there," Colin says with a smile, looking at me first, then at Chloe and Georgia.

Well, isn't this nice and AWKWARD.

OMG could this get any weirder
I feel like I'm always in the middle of some
LucyGeorgiaSoapOpera sandwich
T.G. this isn't my afterlife.

Chloe's got that right. My afterlife? IS a soap opera.

"Hey," I say.

Chloe and Georgia just stand there silently.

"I was going to see if I could walk you to gym, but it looks like you already have escorts," he says, chuckling.

Just then Miles rounds the same corner, and the five of us collide.

Like a million alternate universes.

Or a terrible, terrible car accident where no one comes out alive.

(You know what I mean.)

"Hey, I—" he says, looking straight at me, but then takes in all the eyes around him and abruptly stops talking.

"Hey," I say back.

It's clear that Miles wanted to find me to tell me something, but obviously "Hey, I" isn't much of a clue.

Even for a psychological spy such as myself.

Colin's eyes flutter down to my neck.

Well she's wearing the necklace
That's a good sign but I don't understand why Miles is
always around
I guess that's probably how she feels about Georgia
I just wish we could make this official already
I'm tired of playing games.

Georgia doesn't miss his subtle glance either, and her eyes follow his until they land squarely on my neck.

"Pretty necklace, Lucy," she says to make things super-duper ridiculously uncomfortable.

THIS? Is the Georgia I know and love to hate.

"Thanks," I say, and I want to stop there, but the look on Colin's face is begging for me to give him credit. To say it out loud. And he deserves that. After all, I know what he wants now. He just thought it. (Even though I'm not supposed to be listening to people's thoughts, it's impossible to help it.) He wants us to be official. To be together. And isn't that what *I've* been wanting since the day I crossed over?

"Colin gave it to me, actually," I reply, and as I say it, my right hand drifts up to finger the charm, like I'm protecting it from her or something.

Here. We. Go . . .

Georgia's face goes from normal to DEFCON 1 in 3.5 seconds. It gets redder than a chili pepper, and her eyes widen as if they're about to implode. She has enough pent-up anger inside her to start smoking.

Literally.

I can't believe this is happening
Why does this girl get everything she wants
I don't understand it Even after I tricked Miles into showing up
at the arcade to ruin her date with Colin she still got away with
everything and they both still love her what is it about her I'm
so angry I could scream I can't handle this anymore if I don't
leave here I'm going to explode!!!!!!!!!!!!!!!!!

Whoa. Okay, I know I wanted to break down her Wall, but I didn't actually want to break *her*.

Just then Georgia sigh-screams and storms off in a huff toward the gym. Chloe raises an eyebrow as if to say, *Here we go again!* and follows suit.

And then there were three.

I can't believe Georgia really did it! She actually tricked Miles into coming to the arcade! I have proof now! Well, proof locked up inside Georgia's head.

I mean, I thought it was her, but I don't know if I *really* thought it was her, you know? Part of me wanted it to be her because I didn't want to be stupid enough to have made the mistake myself without even realizing it, but she and I were just starting to be friends. How nice that would have been . . . And instead, she stabbed me in the back. Again. And hurt poor Miles in the process. What did he ever do to her?!

"I'll see you later," Miles says quietly, and breaks away from us, heading back in the direction he came from.

And then there were two.

I can't blame Miles for leaving. After all, we were just standing here in a totally icky silence while I ran through the train wreck of thoughts in my head.

That can't be very exciting to outsiders.

Unless, of course, he can *hear* me . . .

Why oh why is this happening to me?? What is it that Miles wanted to say to me? Was it important? Could he have wanted to say something personal—something about us? But what about Briana? Maybe he wanted to tell me they're officially dating? UGH, I'm so confused. Ooh! Maybe it was about the whole telepathy thing?

I need to find out.

Meanwhile, Colin is just standing there, staring at me, waiting for me to say something, but I'm at a loss.

"That was fun, huh?" he says finally, trying to lighten the mood.

If there's one thing I can say for Colin, he does always make me laugh.

"The MOST fun I've ever had," I agree, chuckling a little.

"Are you okay?" he asks.

I wonder what exactly he means by this. Is he asking me because of Georgia's reaction? Or what she might do next? Or because of Miles?

"I'm okay," I say.

"I'm really happy you're wearing the necklace," he says. "It looks nice on you."

"I love it. I really do."

"So . . . since you're wearing it, does this mean that, you know, we're actually doing this?"

OMG. This is it. The moment of truth. Colin is finally asking me if I want to be his girlfriend. I think. That's what he means, right? What else could he mean? He said he wanted it to be official inside his head, so that must be what he means.

And I can't hesitate, because hesitating is the kiss of death. Pun intended!

AHHHHHHHHHHHHHHHHHHHHHHHHHH!

"Do *you* want to be doing this?" I ask, just to triple-check.

"This as in *us*?" he says.

"Isn't that what you meant?" I confirm.

Jeez, we're a regular stand-up routine. It's like we're playing that improvisation game where you can only answer a question with a question.

"Is that what you want it to mean?" he answers.

"We should go on tour," I say finally, too frustrated to continue.

Briiiiiing! Briiiiiing!

You have GOT to be kidding me.

"Sorry, I'm just . . . a little nervous," he says, brushing his hand through his hair. The silver ring glimmers in the hallway light. "Yes, I meant we're doing this as in we're officially an us. And yes, that's what I want."

"Me too," I say finally.

"Okay, good."

"Okay, good."

"I better go," I say. "That was the second bell; we'll both be in trouble."

"It's worth it," he replies, smiling. "I'll see you in a bit."

"Okay, see you."

We part ways, and I head into P.E., where a psychotic Georgia is waiting for me.

Awesome.

My brain is officially on overload. Me and Colin are an US. I have a boyfriend. Me. Lucy. And it's Colin.

AHHHHHHHHHHHHHHHHHHHHHH!

And I finally got Georgia to lose control so much that her Wall crumbled down and out tumbled a GALLON of mean-girl juice. The girl Hates me, with a capital *H*. And why? Is it my fault that two boys happen to like me? There are a million other ghosts at this school she could like! Fine, Colin is her ex. Okay, I get it. But she treated him terribly. And it's over between them.

O.V.E.R.

Everyone has to move on eventually!

I walk into the gym, and we've already been split up into teams for dodgeball.

Of course we HAVE to be playing a game with balls today. Just my luck.

"Lucy, you're late!" Coach Trellis calls.

"I'm sorry!" I squeal, hoping she'll give me a pass.

"Next time I'm sending you to the principal's office."

"It won't happen again!"

"Go ahead, join the blue team."

Georgia and I are on opposite teams, giving her ample opportunities to throw the ball repeatedly at my head. Or at any other body part she chooses.

Except this time, I'm a tougher target. It *is* called dodgeball for a reason.

I'm managing to fend off her tosses well, but she certainly is LASER-focused on pounding me into the ground.

She's not hiding her disdain either. Everyone is looking at one another, wondering what in Limbo they stepped into.

This? Is a war zone.

And without Chloe as her sidekick this time to help mask her intentions, this personal vendetta of hers is on the front lines.

"Georgia, why don't you try throwing the ball at someone other than Lucy for a change?" Coach Trellis calls out, because even she realizes there's more than meets the eye here.

Georgia acquiesces for a few minutes, and then goes right back to targeting yours truly. Finally, out of pure exhaustion, I lose focus for a hot second and—

WHAM!!!!!!

Right at my head.

Again.

"Foul!" Coach Trellis calls out. (At least she saw it this time.) "Georgia, go to the bench and take a time-out. Lucy, are you okay? Do you need to go to the nurse's office?"

"I'm fine, Coach, thanks," I say, rubbing my head.

The rest of the period goes by without much drama, given that Georgia's on the bench, far away from me, but I can feel her eyes slicing into me like knives. Forget about breaking the Wall—I've opened the floodgates.

And you know what? It's time for me to fight it. Once and for all.

Always raise the stakes, right?

The bell rings and everyone heads for the door, including Georgia, who is the first one out. I dart down the hallway after her until I reach her locker, where we both stop.

"So much for wiping the slate clean, huh?" I say angrily.

"You should talk," she replies. "Kind of two-faced to tell me you want to be friends one minute and then start dating my ex-boyfriend LITERALLY the next minute."

"You guys broke up!" I exclaim. "I know it for a fact this time."

The hallway is bustling with people going from third to fourth period now, and no one is even trying to look away.

This fight? Is center stage.

"When was the last time you broke up with someone, Lucy?" Georgia asks, almost calmly.

I stay quiet, because the answer is *never*.

"That's what I thought. Since you have absolutely no experience in this area whatsoever, allow me to enlighten you: Just because you break up with someone, that doesn't mean everything suddenly gets wiped clean. Feelings don't just disappear the moment you want them to. Especially if you didn't see the breakup coming. Like, say, if out of nowhere someone new shows up and ruins everything for you when you thought things were going great. Perfect, even."

Georgia looks down at her feet, and once again, for a split second, the other Georgia—the real one, maybe?—shines through.

And I actually feel sorry for her.

"So," I say quietly, "you think that if I hadn't shown up at Limbo, you and Colin would still be living happily ever after together?"

Georgia looks up at me. "Yes, okay? I do. Before you showed up? We were happy. And now I'm stuck in this weird love triangle with you and Colin, who couldn't seem to make up his mind about what he wanted . . . at least not until now."

Her eyes drift over to my neck again, and I realize it was the necklace that made her finally realize it's over. Really over.

He never gave me a necklace.
Why wasn't I good enough?

"So you see, Lucy," she goes on, standing a bit taller now and obviously trying to pull herself back together, "you may not have gotten the starring role in *Twelfth Night*, but you're Viola in real afterlife. Colin used to want me, but then you show up and now he wants you. And I'm old news. Are you happy now?"

I stand there in silence for a moment, just staring. It's like time has stopped, and even though there are people all over the hallway, it feels like it's just me and Georgia, facing off, like we're in some old Western movie or something.

"I never thought about it that way," I say, because it's true. "And I'm sorry that this whole thing has hurt you so much—I really am. But just because things didn't work out the way you planned, it doesn't mean that you get to manipulate and mess with people's lives any way you choose."

I have to stand up for myself. Even though she's hurting, her behavior is SO not okay.

"I know you were the one who sabotaged my date with Colin at the arcade," I continue. "It was you who tricked Miles into showing up."

Georgia looks straight at me, and her eyes widen with surprise. She didn't think I'd figure it out.

"You deserved it," Georgia says flatly.

"No, actually, I didn't. But even if I did, Miles *definitely* didn't. What do you have against him? What did he ever do to you? You could have really embarrassed him and hurt his feelings, and for what?"

"Yeah, well," she says, looking down again, "not everything is personal. It's like I said before, sometimes you do things—"

"Yeah, I know," I say, "for the 'greater good.' The question is, whose good is it for, really? Seems like you're doing it for your own good, and no one else's."

Georgia doesn't say anything else, and neither do I. I do, however, take this moment to look around the hallway to see who has gathered around us.

The answer? Everyone.

All eyes on us.

Particularly Colin and Miles.

Oh goody.

"So it was all just part of your act, then?" I ask her finally.

"Was what all part of my act?"

"Pretending to bury the hatchet, going shopping for friendship souvenirs? The sleepover invite?"

"No, that was real," she says. "But then Colin asked you out and you said yes. And friends don't do that to each other."

At that moment, Georgia takes a book out of her locker, slams the door shut, and just walks away, leaving me standing there with a crowd of people.

Mic drop.

And the truth is? She's right about that. Friends don't do that to each other. Maybe I was kidding myself thinking that Georgia and I were becoming friends. After all, I never would have done this to Cecily or Mia. So she has a point. I concede. I chose Colin over her, and she has a right to be angry and question my loyalty as a friend. And I guess, even though I was willing to give her a second chance, in the end I didn't really trust her so much either.

But I hoped she could change, and isn't that what counts?

I wanted her to change. And she could have, if she wanted to. She could have handled this whole situation very differently, but she didn't. She did the same old thing Georgia always does.

I guess that means we're taking this scene from the top.

As in, Lucy and Mean Girl's Adventures in the Afterlife.

Act 1, Scene 1.

And . . . action.

THE PRINCIPAL RULES OF STAGE ACTING

RULE #8:

Show it, don't tell it.

Chapter Ten
Showtime

After "THE FACE-OFF," which is what everyone at school is now calling my fight with Georgia, I skipped fourth period and went to the nurse's office to lie down.

I did get hit in the ball with a head, remember?

(Oops. I got hit in the *head* with a *ball*. You know what I mean.)

Anyway, I needed to clear my head (the inside!) a bit and get away from everyone. All this talk—and all those thoughts—about me wanting to be the center of attention and loving being in the spotlight or whatever—have got me feeling unsettled. Georgia thought—probably still thinks— I'm some spotlight-craving, self-obsessed Malvolio type. Oliver thought I was jealous of him and Cecily. Even Cecily thought I created this story about Georgia to drum up drama because I couldn't stand that she was getting more attention than me.

And that? Makes my head spin.

Maybe Cecily was right. Maybe I did get too caught up in the play and lose sight of what was real and what wasn't. Because the truth is that normally, I HATE being in the spotlight.

HATE it with all capital letters.

It's my absolute least favorite kind of light to be in!

Seriously.

I'd take sunlight, flashlight, daylight, candlelight, moonlight—I'd even take a stoplight—over the spotlight any day of the week.

So . . . how did this happen? And what do I do now?

Briiiiing! Briiiiing!

Great, that's the second bell for fifth period, which means I need to report to the auditorium to get into makeup and costume for the play.

So much for making a game plan.

I get up, head out of the nurse's office, and make my way toward the auditorium. I run into Miles again just as I'm approaching the front doors.

Is fate trying to tell us something or what?

"Hey!" I say, surprised by how relieved I am to see him. "I've been wanting to talk to you for hours."

"Hey," he says with that same exact even-keeled voice as always.

"Listen, I'm sorry things were so weird before P.E. when you came to talk to me."

"No worries."

A man of few words.

"And I'm really sorry about what you may have overheard in the hallway between me and Georgia."

"What I *may* have overheard?" He smirks.

I smile back. He's trying to get me to just come out and say it, and I have to respect him for it.

"Fine, I'm sorry that you had to find out that Georgia is the one who invited you to the arcade on Saturday—not me—from our stupid fight in the hallway. I'm sorry that it happened at all, and I'm really sorry that I didn't just tell you about it on Saturday night, or any other day after that. I just . . . I didn't want to hurt your feelings."

"Is that really why?" he asks.

"I mean, it's partially why. I also like spending time with you, so there's that."

"Okay. Is that all?"

He's still incredibly calm, and I can't tell how he's feeling about anything.

Talk about a poker face.

"I guess not," I continue. "I guess I should also tell you that Colin and I are officially, you know, together, or whatever, just so there's no confusion."

"Okay."

"Can you please say something else? Something that resembles any kind of actual feeling or statement?"

At this he laughs. Not a rude or hurtful laugh, a genuine you're-so-ridiculous-I'm-laughing kind of laugh.

"I'm so glad I amuse you," I say with a smirk.

"I'm sorry," he says. "I couldn't help myself. What I came to tell you earlier, when I walked into some weird *Twilight Zone*–type wormhole, is that I know you're a telepath, because I'm one too. And if you want someone to talk to about it, I'm around."

OMG. Half of me is ecstatic right now, and half of me is totally and completely bummed. And mortified.

Maybe Miles never even liked me in the first place? Maybe I just made it all up in my head because I wanted him to?

"Oh, wow. Okay, cool, great. That's great. So, uhm, how did you find out about me?"

"When we took a walk that day at lunch. I don't use the power too often because we're not supposed to; plus, I don't really care what most other people are thinking—and honestly, it's more of a pain than a benefit, at least around here. But you had been acting so strange, and you seemed to know things I was thinking, so I allowed myself to listen, just to see. And you came through loud and clear."

"So you heard what I was thinking?"

"Yeah. I knew you lied to me about Cecily before, but that day I found out why."

"And you put up your Wall when you realized what was happening?"

"Someone's been reading up," he says. "Look, just be careful, okay? Don't be too obvious about it, and try not to listen in on people too much. I can help you block some of the voices out if you want. Listening in on other people's thoughts can get you into trouble, you know?"

"Oh, boy, do I ever."

"Besides, as you probably expected, there are a lot of rules at Limbo Central about telepathy. You're not even supposed to be able to access your powers if you have any until at least Year Three. Not that I'm surprised you're ahead of the game, though," he says, shrugging and offering me a sweet smile.

"Thanks."

At that moment, Cecily and Oliver burst out of the auditorium doors in costume and appear by our side.

"We were just coming to look for you, Lou!" Cecily says.

"Wow, you guys look great!" I cry, surprised. We haven't done a full dress rehearsal, so this is the first time I'm seeing them in costume.

"We heard about your head," Cecily goes on. "Are you okay?"

"My head?" I say, and it takes me a minute to realize they're referring to the ball that Georgia threw at it. "Oh, right. Well, my head's a little off, but I'll be okay, I think."

I toss a quick wink at Miles.

Just then I hear this:

Good luck with the play
But you probably don't need any
I'm sure you're a natural.

Miles is talking to me—WITH HIS MIND!

I look back at him, and think:

Well I'm no Olivia.

He smiles and starts to walk away. As he does, he calls out, "No, you certainly aren't."

I can't tell if that's a good thing or a bad thing, but I do know I'm not supposed to care. I'm with Colin now, so I need to just put all this Miles stuff behind me.

Or away in a drawer.

And lock it.

And choose a ridiculously long passcode that I won't write down anywhere so I'll never remember it.

"Uhm, hello?" Oliver shouts down the hall toward Miles. "What am I, *invisible*?!"

"Good luck, little brother!" Miles shouts back.

"It's BREAK A LEG!" Oliver screams. "Why doesn't anyone here know that?!"

"We can't all be as posh and in-the-know as you are." I give him my best innocent face.

"I suppose that's true," he says. "Anyway, what was *THAT* about?"

"I was just apologizing to him for the whole Georgia thing."

"That girl definitely has her claws in you," he says. Then his expression changes and gets serious, which for Oliver is, like, unheard of. "Listen, I just wanted to say I'm sorry, you know, for letting this play get the better of me. We were kind of being our own little clique of two this week, totally wrapped up in the play, and I let the drama spiral outward. You know what they say, 'All the world's a stage, and all the men and women are merely players!'"

"Wrong play, Ollie," Cecily says. "That's *As You Like It*."

"Is that by Shakespeare?" he asks, exasperated, as if the two of them are some kind of married couple.

"Yes," Cecily offers.

"Then it counts!" he replies, triumphant. "Now, where was I. Oh yes. Will you please, please forgive us?"

"Of course!" I announce happily.

I glance over at Cecily, and she looks like she's about to cry.

"I'm so sorry, Lou. I can't believe I didn't believe you when you told me about Georgia," she says.

"It's okay," I answer, putting my arm around her. And I mean it. "I know it sounded insane, and you were right to question it. I haven't exactly been my normal self since this play started, either. Which reminds me, I'm also very sorry I blew up at both of you in the hall that day. I guess I was a little bit jealous, which is embarrassing to admit, but it's true. But I can honestly say that I'm SO happy I don't have either of your parts, and I have absolutely no interest in being the star of this show."

"Apology accepted!" Oliver says. "Now it's time for THIS star to go get into character!"

With that, he heads straight back through the auditorium doors and leaves the two of us alone.

"I mean it, Lou, I'm really sorry," Cecily says again. "There I was accusing you of getting too caught up in the play, when I was the one doing that! I was so obsessed with being the best and showing everyone I deserved the lead that I completely lost sight of everything else. And I wasn't there for you. I feel awful."

"But you *were* there for me! You were there for me big-time Saturday night when I needed help."

"Yeah, but not when you needed help with Georgia."

"If you were there every time I needed help with Georgia, you literally wouldn't be able to get anything done EVER," I say, chuckling. "Besides, you had a lot on your mind. You're the lead in the play! That's HUGE! And it's literally less than an hour till showtime, so stop talking to me about this and go get ready!!"

I think about telling Cecily that I'm a telepath, but decide not to. At least, I decide not to tell her now. I'm sure at some-time in the future I'll reveal it, but now is not the right time. For one, she's got WAY too much on her mind. For another, I'd like to keep this one to myself for a little while longer.

We head into the auditorium, up the stairs to the stage, and go backstage where everyone is getting ready.

There are tights and hats and ribbons flying everywhere, and Lana Polasky is running around with a clipboard, screaming at people.

"This bodice is way too tight!" Briana yells at Lana as she passes by.

"Just hold your breath!" Lana replies. "And, Lucy, get yourself over to costume—now!"

"Have you ever seen anything this chaotic in your life?" Mia says, appearing by our sides.

"Well, don't you look handsome, Sir Belch," I say.

"Yes, I feel rather dashing," she replies.

"I feel like I might throw up," Cecily says.

"You're not going to throw up," I say calmly. "You're going to be great! You know this part backward and forward. And inside out. You ARE Viola! Now go get a glass of water or something and sit down. I better go get dressed or Lana will have my head."

I hurry over to the fitting room as Ms. Barnard comes rushing through the crowd.

"We have exactly thirty-five minutes till curtain!" she calls out to us. "I hope everyone is excited! Remember to leave it all out on stage! That's why we call it *show*time, not *tell*time!"

On my way to wardrobe, I spot Colin. He's already dressed, and I can't deny he looks very, very cute in his lordly garb.

"Well, if it isn't Sir Sebastian," I say, smirking. "You're looking very noble."

"That's only because I have such a fair lady by my side," he replies, an overly corny expression across his face.

I giggle. "Except for the fact that I'm not actually a lady, well, not for much longer anyway."

"Lucy!" Lana belts out, darting past us yet again. "You have three minutes to get into costume!"

"Right," Colin says. "Well, you're a lady for the next three minutes, anyway, and that's what's important, because see, I was hoping to be able to give my lady a good-luck kiss."

I overtly blush, and immediately try to cover it up with my hands and fail.

MISERABLY.

"Lucy, seriously!" Lana cries out. "Two minutes!"

It's like she has nothing better to do but stalk me?! I roll my eyes, offer Colin my best apologetic look, and begin to walk away.

But then think better of it. "Hey, before I go, can I ask you a question?"

"You can ask me anything."

"Were you happy with Georgia? I mean, before I crossed over? Like, were you really happy together?"

Colin chuckles to himself and looks down at his hands. He's taken his ring off for the play, but I can still see the tan line from where the sun tinted his skin around it.

"Let's put it this way: Think of me as Orsino. Orsino was pretty sure he was in love with Olivia before Viola arrived, but does that mean he really was? Or that he just didn't know someone else could make him happier?"

"Good answer," I say, because it is.

"Break a leg out there."

"You too," I reply, and I give him a soft kiss on the cheek.

"Lucy, NOW!" Lana belts out.

"I'm going, I'm going!"

Jeez, theater types are so sensitive.

I enter the fitting room, slip on my Malvolio costume, and try to get into character. All right . . . who *is* Malvolio? Hmmmm, let's see: Hostile. Dishonest. Snobbish. Resentful. Self-righteous. Gold digger. Egotistic.

That's right, how could I forget?

But you know what? It's totally and completely fine. I have no problem being Malvolio anymore. You know why?

Because if this play has taught me anything, it's that the only role that truly matters is the one I play in afterlife. After all, it's easy to be a perfect leading lady on stage when everything is written line by line and all you need to do is memorize it! Of course, I'm NOT a leading lady on stage, but you know what I mean.

It's a metaphor, people!

Being a good person in real afterlife—doing the right thing even when it's hard, being good to the people I love and care about, and even sacrificing my own happiness for someone else's because they deserve it more—that can be tricky sometimes. Because it's not like the steps are written out for me to follow. I just have to do what I think is best.

And sometimes I get it wrong; we all do. But a lot of times I get it right, because I follow my heart—my non-beating, non-bleeding, for-all-intents-and-purposes-totally-for-show heart.

You get the sentiment.

And you know what else? I think Shakespeare was wrong about one thing. That line Oliver said earlier, "All the world's a stage, and all the men and women are merely players"? Well, I don't agree with that. I mean, the world might be a stage, but I don't want to be a player. I want to be real.

SO.

Here are *MY* Principal Rules for my very REAL afterlife:

Rule #1: I, Lucy Lou Chadwick, vow to trust my instincts, because they are usually right. And even when they aren't, I'll still trust them, because everyone needs to make mistakes.

Rule #2: I reserve the right to *rewrite* my lines at any point in time! And the roles of any of the people in my afterlife, because everyone deserves a do-over.

Rule #3: I intend to be believable because I *actually* believe in what I'm doing or saying, not because I'm a good actress. (Which clearly I'm not. And no, I'm *NOT* being bitter or dramatic about it.)

Rule #4: Sometimes I'm going to know the "structure" of how things will play out, and sometimes I won't. And that's OKAY.

Rule #5: Listening is a good rule, so I'll keep that one. But not when it applies to telepathy. (At least not until I learn more about how to control it.)

Rule #6: Sometimes I'll eat my ego, and sometimes I won't. For example, when it comes to standing up for myself and what I believe in. Especially against the newly reinstated Georgia McMean Face.

Rule #7: I guess raising the stakes is okay sometimes, so I'll leave this one in on a provisionary basis.

And finally . . .

Rule #8: I, Lucy Lou Chadwick, vow to show things when I want to show them and tell things when I want to tell them, and I also reserve the right to think things when I don't feel like telling them or showing them.

So there.

"Okay, it's time, everyone!" Ms. Barnard whisper-screams as we all take our places on stage. "Everyone break a leg, and don't forget to have fun out there!"

Three. Two. One.

Curtain!

Don't miss a minute in Limbo!

Happily Ever Afterlife #1:
Ghostcoming!

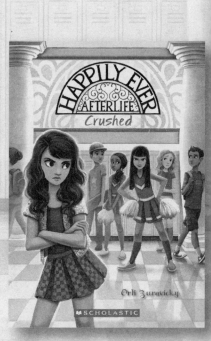

Happily Ever Afterlife #2:
Crushed

Read the latest *wish* books!

donut go breaking my heart

Graceful

WENDY MASS

ANGELA CERVANTES

ALLIE FIRST AT LAST

carolyn mackler

best friend next door

TWICE UPON A TIME

Rapunzel

The One with All the Hair

WENDY MASS

deep down popular

PHOEBE STONE

REVENGE OF THE **ANGELS**

JENNIFER ZIEGLER

Natalie Blitt

CAROLS AND CRUSHES

Sealed with a Secret

LISA SCHROEDER

SCHOLASTIC

scholastic.com/Wish

WISHSUMFALL16

Orli Zuravicky is a writer, an editor, and an amateur interior designer, which basically means she likes to paint stuff in her apartment. She has been in children's publishing for fifteen years and has written over sixty-five books for children. She hopes to write sixty-five more. She lives her happily ever after (life) in Brooklyn, New York.